FROST FIRE

Jamie Smith

Chicken House

2 PALMER STREET, FROME, SOMERSET BA11 1DS

Text © Jamie Smith 2018

First published in Great Britain in 2018
Chicken House
2 Palmer Street
Frome, Somerset BA11 1DS
United Kingdom
www.chickenhousebooks.com

Jamie Smith has asserted his right under the Copyright, Designs and
Patents Act 1988 to be identified as the author of this work.

Cover and interior design by Steve Wells
Cover and interior illustrations by Karl James Mountford
Typeset by Dorchester Typesetting Group Ltd
Printed and bound in Great Britain by CPI Group (UK) Ltd, Croydon CR0 4YY

The paper used in this Chicken House book is made
from wood grown in sustainable forests.

1 3 5 7 9 10 8 6 4 2

British Library Cataloguing in Publication data available.

PB ISBN 978-1-911077-87-9
eISBN 978-1-911490-65-4

PART I

PROLOGUE

The mountain had murder in mind.

That was the only explanation for the howling wind, the savage pinpricks of hail and the shifting snow underfoot. Sabira held a gloved hand in front of her face and pushed on up the sheer steps cut into the rock, her leg muscles screaming. It felt like they'd been climbing for ever.

The steps had no handrail, and the drop churned her stomach. Rather than risk staring into it, Sabira kept her focus on Uncle Mihnir's broad back. Further ahead, Frost-Cleric Tserah walked through the gale as if the harsh climb was no more than a stroll through the lowlands in summer.

She couldn't be afraid. Not here, not now. She'd been chosen because Tserah thought she was smart and strong; only one in every hundred who came of age were judged worthy of a visit to the glacier. She should be proud.

So why did it feel more like a curse than a blessing?

Abruptly, Tserah crested the steps and waited for the others to catch up. She was impressive, standing straight against the wind. Shades of scarlet cleric's robes showed through gaps in her furs – and near her neckline, Sabira glimpsed a soft blue glow. Her frost-sliver. Soon she would have one of her own, Sabira thought, touching the empty necklace hanging around at her throat. She wouldn't fail.

As Sabira and her uncle reached the top, Mihnir pointed towards the mountain peak and shouted over the wind: 'Storm's coming in – a real one, not like this drizzle!' Heavy furs accentuated his already large, rounded frame; he looked more like a cave bear than a person.

Looking over her shoulder, Sabira wished she could see Adranna's icy walls glinting in the sunshine, but the huge rocky overhang that shielded her home city from weather also hid it from her now. Sabira's gaze strayed to the other side of the ridge, to where the glacier flowed down the mountainside, a great tongue of ice. It wound away into the distance, towards the place where she knew it tipped off the mountain, its magic melting and diluting into water.

It was certainly no normal glacier: they hardly moved if you spent a day watching. But the Tears of Aderast flowed at a clear walking pace, and had a slight sapphire glow, like the cleric's frostsliver. The light of magic, the flame with no heat. Frostfire. Lines of scarlet prayer flags fluttered and danced in the gale nearby, straining on their moorings and threatening to rip away. Sabira's heart fluttered with them.

'Maybe we should turn back!' Mihnir called.

Sabira glanced at her uncle. She couldn't bear the thought of descending the bonding path to the city, only to climb it again once the storm had passed. 'I'll be quick,' she shouted. Both of them looked to the frost-cleric for a decision.

To Sabira's relief, Tserah nodded.

This was the final leg of Sabira's journey, and by tradition it had to be travelled alone. She gulped and watched the slow-moving glacier for a few moments, as though it had frozen her in place.

Tserah laid a white-furred glove on Sabira's shoulder and squeezed in encouragement, just before Mihnir pulled her into a suffocating hug. She pressed her nose into his furs and blinked to stop her eyes stinging. She couldn't tighten her arms around the whole of his large frame, but she really tried.

'Don't worry about . . .' he said, and then started again. 'You'll be fine, just keep your head on what you're doing.'

He smiled at her as he pulled away. Mihnir should know. As a packman, he had brought more potential bonders here than anyone. Sabira nodded, but couldn't speak. Her nerves were too high, and even in the penetrating cold, she could feel the heat of her quick heartbeat. Then, just as she had been about to put a foot forward, a different voice broke in – not Tserah's calm, hard tone, or Uncle Mihnir's jolly one. It was a strange voice, like the ringing of a crystal glass gently touched.

I hope my kin are happy with you.

Sabira jumped at the sound, for there was no one but the three of them there. Except, of course, there was another as well, hanging around Tserah's neck. Her fraction of the mountain god. Her frostsliver. This was the first time it had spoken to Sabira – they rarely talked to anyone they were not bonded with.

'Thank you, I think,' said Sabira, looking at Tserah, for the cleric's senses were shared with her bonded frostsliver. Tserah smiled and touched her hand to the blue glow in her clothes.

They all seemed to have such confidence in her. It scared Sabira. Her life had been full of uncertainty and it was hard to believe that now would be different. She turned to face the last stretch of the path, the glacier clouded by fog. For a moment, she stood still, gathering her courage.

This was it. This was where she followed in the footsteps of every Aderasti that had come before . . . and the footsteps of her brother, Kyran. She blinked away a tear. She didn't feel ready at all.

Sabira took her first step.

CHAPTER ONE

One year earlier

'How much longer?' Sabira asked. She and her parents stood on top of the ice wall surrounding the city, waiting. She walked to the edge of the wall, peered briefly down into the valley. She spun on her heels, turning towards the mountain and the shrine for the hundredth time, half expecting her brother to emerge at last. But the path remained empty. She took a few steps and turned again to the valley.

'He's going to be fine, either way,' her father said soothingly. 'You don't have to pace like that while you're waiting. What are you going to be like when I go off in a few weeks' time? It'll be for months, you know.'

Sabira's father was a respected healer and had been invited on an important diplomatic trip to Ignata. Sabira shook her head. 'This is different. This is Kyran's whole future at stake,' she said, walking faster than ever.

'It *would* be easier if they told us the schedule,' said Taranna, her mother. She was anxious too, but instead of pacing, she fiddled with the two red ribbons on her upper arm – representing her two children. Her father had identical ribbons tied around his arm. 'Your father's right, Sabira. Stop pacing. You're making me even more nervous.'

Sabira stopped and sighed. They waited along with a few other family groups near the frost-cleric temple where Sabira had her lessons, its great glass greenhouse and domed observatory glinting in the sunlight. It was Choosing Day, and along with the other children of Adranna who had reached the age of fourteen, Sabira's brother was undergoing tests to determine if he was worthy of bonding a frostsliver.

Only one in a hundred were destined to succeed, but Sabira thought they'd choose Kyran. He was strong and clever and everything a big brother should be. He'd climb up to the glacier above on Aderast's highest slopes and cut a piece of it for himself, a piece of a god to grant him the powers he'd always dreamt about. She just wished she knew it for sure.

'So . . . how much longer *can* it be?' Sabira asked, jittering in place as she stared at her scuffed snow boots on the painted ice.

'Look!' her mother said, pointing up to the shrine.

A figure had emerged from the low, peak-roofed building: Kyran. He strode down towards their parents, and Sabira felt her heart thumping as she tried to read his expression for an answer. Suddenly, to Sabira's eyes, he looked very grown up – even though he was only one year older than her. He hesitated in front of his family.

'Well?' said Sabira's father.

'Yeah,' he eventually said, almost in a whisper. 'They picked me. I'm going to have a frostsliver!' A smile broke across his face.

Her mother and father cried out, scooping Sabira and Kyran into a tight embrace. Sabira clung to her brother. All sorts of feelings ran through her in a shiver. Joy for the magic that had come into Kyran's life, the magic he'd longed for since he was a small boy. Pride for the older brother she loved. A little bit of jealousy that he was the one who'd been chosen, not her. Worry for him making the dangerous climb up the bonding path.

'That's amazing, son,' said their father, pulling away, his eyes shining.

'Well done, Kyran. Well done,' their mother added,

squeezing Kyran's shoulder as she released him.

But Sabira didn't let go. She could feel her eyes stinging. 'Hey, what's wrong?' Kyran asked, concerned, prising her away gently.

'You're really going . . . up there to the glacier?' Sabira asked haltingly. 'Some people don't come back.'

'*I'll* come back!' Kyran replied, full of confidence. 'You don't have to worry about me.'

Sabira's parents walked ahead, leaving her and Kyran wandering down towards the city as the sun started to sink. For a while, they were quiet, each lost in their own thoughts.

'I guess in all the excitement it feels like your birthday has been forgotten,' he said quietly.

Sabira blinked. She'd even forgotten herself: she was thirteen today. 'It doesn't matter. Your Choosing is more important,' she said sincerely.

'Of course it matters. You're thirteen now – that means you've only got one more year left until your own Choosing. Have you thought about it yet, about what you want?'

Sabira shrugged. She had thought about her own Choosing – of course she had. But it had always felt so distant, like a daydream. Now, her stomach clenched in nervousness. What if she wasn't good enough for a frostsliver? What if she *was*?

'Anyway, as you've only got one year of official

childhood left, I thought I'd give you something special.' He reached into his pocket and drew something out. 'Happy birthday, Sabira.' He handed her a small wooden figurine, hand-carved and smooth. Sabira took the creature. To her surprise, it had little posable legs, so you could make the figurine stand or sit. It had a long, lithe body and a fierce face.

'Is it an ash-cat?' she asked, grinning. Her brother nodded.

'I made it myself,' he said, a little shyly. 'I know how curious you are about Ignata.'

'I love it!' she said, hugging him for the second time that afternoon. 'Thank you!'

He squeezed her back.

When she pulled away, she cradled the ash-cat carefully in her hand as they carried on walking home. 'Everything's changing, isn't it? You'll have your frostsliver. Father's going to leave on the Ignatian delegation in a few weeks . . . soon it will just be me and Mother.' Sabira felt a sharp tug in her heart at the thought. She loved her mother, of course, but it would be weird with the family cut in half.

'It'll be all right. Think of everything I'll be able to achieve once I'm bonded!' Kyran's eyes grew suddenly dreamy. 'Everyone with a frostsliver does something important. One day, maybe I can go on trips like Father. I bet you could come too, Sabira – we could see the world, from Ignata to the plains nations! Won't you like that? You're always talking about travelling. Maybe you'll have a frostsliver by then too.' He grinned at her. 'You'll see, everything will turn out for the best.'

Sabira smiled. She hoped he was right. Her brother had all the courage in the world, but she wasn't sure if that was enough. Something was niggling at the back of her mind, some darkness or foreboding. Maybe she was worrying over nothing. Yes, that was it. He'd head up the path in a week's time and be home a day or two later, a frostsliver around his neck and magical frostfire running through his fingers, just like he'd always wanted.

CHAPTER TWO

Sabira and Kyran trudged down the slope, watching their mother's back, her bow and quiver of arrows slung across her shoulders. The three of them had set out on a hunting trip to a small forest near the base of the mountain, hoping for a catch to help celebrate Kyran's last meal before he set out for the glacier.

'We'll be there soon.'

Her mother's words startled Sabira from her thoughts. It was her third hunting trip, and this one had to go better than the first two. Sabira had startled everything away the first time, and the second hadn't been much better. Her mother suffered it all with no more than a sigh, though Kyran was less patient. Sabira refused to ruin everything again.

'I'm ready. This time I'll get it right,' she said, following her mother as she picked a path over the rocks.

Kyran snorted, but their mother stopped and turned, expression solemn.

'You're only thirteen, Sabira. This isn't something you should expect to learn quickly. I bungled my first few hunting trips. Most people do,' she said. She shot a stern look at Kyran, adding, 'Even you. And *you* should be taking things more seriously now. You'll have a frostsliver soon – you're going to have to learn some responsibility.'

Sabira and Kyran exchanged grimaces behind their mother's back as she led the way towards the forest.

They were long past the end of Adranna's stone stairway, and almost beyond the rocky scree of the foothills. Grassy shoots poked through the frosty earth, clawing free of their icy prison. Sabira smiled. Only a hint of green ever touched Adranna, but down here sparse bushes and evergreen trees dotted the landscape. It was warm too, despite the breeze. Sabira pulled her heavy furs away from her neck. Perhaps when they reached the forest her mother would let her hide some of her clothes so she didn't cook.

Suddenly, as they started to round a corner, Sabira

14

noticed smoke billowing over the next hillock.

'What's this?' her mother murmured, quickening her pace. Sabira hurried after her, struggling to keep up with Taranna's longer stride. After a minute or two, they rounded the hillock and Sabira's heart plunged.

'It can't be . . .' Kyran breathed, next to her.

The forest was on fire.

Sabira couldn't take it in. Heat washed over her in waves, intense even a few hundred paces from the tree line. Her eyes were wide and stinging. Smoke and ash flew everywhere, sweeping across the ground and filling the sky.

Her mother had stopped, her face pale with horror. 'I need to know what happened,' she said. 'We're going to go a little closer – stay next to me and do what I say, when I say it. I don't want you getting hurt.'

Though Sabira had to force herself to follow, they paced onwards, muffling their mouths to protect themselves. The fire burnt hot, and occasionally a gust of wind blew smoke straight into their faces. Sabira coughed and blinked, keeping low to the ground, Kyran close at her side. Soon, her mother held up a hand to stop, and they just stared, eyes stinging with tears.

Flames licked up tree trunks and along branches, shrivelling and withering the dying wood. The smell of burning flesh was sharp in the air: living things snuffed out by unforgiving fire.

Sabira hated it. She wanted to help, but what could she do? Run for water? Beat out some of the flames? She started forward blindly, but stopped as her mother laid a hand on her shoulder and said, 'There's nothing we can do. We'll have to wait until it burns out on its own.'

They watched, helpless. The dangerous dancing flames were mesmerizing.

'What could do this?' Kyran asked. 'Lightning?'

'Not what – *who*,' her mother replied. 'Get down!' she hissed suddenly. Sabira and Kyran ducked, squinting into the trees in confusion. Eventually, she spotted dark shapes emerging from the grey haze ahead.

People were born from the smoke – twenty or more. Sabira had never seen people like them. Their clothes were furless, unsuited to the mountain weather, and they stank of tar. The people didn't appear to have seen them yet, though that wouldn't last. Each one wore the same black leather uniform. Shiny metal symbols decorated some shoulders in silver or gold, and all had hoods tightly cinched for protection from the smoke. She couldn't see their faces, but from their size and clothing, Sabira guessed they were all men.

The men moved away from the smoke towards where they were hiding, Sabira's heart beating to their pace. Did they really start this fire? They must have been careless. Let a campfire get out of control.

They were holding muskets. She glanced at Kyran, knowing they were realizing the same thing.

They're Ignatians.

The men started pushing back their hoods. Their skin was a shade different, and they didn't have rosy Aderasti cheeks either. They had harsh, angular features, and their eyes were hidden under black crystal goggles. Maybe it was to save their vision from the smoke, but it made them look monstrous, empty of emotion.

'By the lash, that's better. Smells like home now,' said one of them.

That's when Sabira knew: they had done this on purpose. She felt cold with anger.

The speaker was short and bulky, and had silver symbols pinned to his shoulders. His lower lip had a deep slice out of one side, as if he had been cut long ago with a hot knife, the edges of the wound healed jagged and red. He had a strange accent but though Sabira almost didn't want to, she did understand him.

She could feel the danger here – they had to leave. Her mother was already slinking backwards, signalling Sabira and Kyran to do the same – but as Sabira followed, a twig cracked under her heel. The squat, silver-shouldered man shouted, 'Colonel Yupin! Look!'

He pointed at them with a thickly muscled arm. Sabira felt a stab of fear in her stomach, hotter than the fire. She started to run, but her mother grabbed her by the wrist. 'No, Sabira – they have muskets,' she said, her voice taut. Silently, Kyran held Sabira's other hand.

Another, taller man with gold symbols on his shoulders fixed his black eyes upon them. 'Well spotted, Sergeant Major,' Yupin said.

Colonel Yupin's head was shaven, like most of the others, and his cheeks were gaunt. Under each eye, tiny symbols had been blackened on to his skin. Sabira couldn't make out any meaning – her people and theirs spoke the same words, but wrote with different letters. She was glad of that – she didn't want to know what a man like this would write on himself.

'Move in,' he said, barely glancing at his men.

The other Ignatians seemed almost as scared of him as Sabira was. They flinched when he looked in their direction, even though he seemed to be the only one of them unarmed.

'Stay behind me,' her mother said, shielding her children from the advancing men, who quickly encircled them. Sabira's heart was pounding, but she forced herself to stand still. Kyran held her hand tightly and shot her a small smile – as if telling her that everything would be all right.

Drawing herself tall in the tendrils of smoke, their mother raised her voice. 'Yupin? Why have you done this?' she asked, her words ringing out over the crackling of the forest fire. She said his name like she knew the man.

'We do as we please with our land, Aderasti,' the squat sergeant major answered for his master. Sabira quaked with worry, but her mother showed no fear.

'This is not your land. What do you mean by this? Is it some kind of warning?'

Although she addressed Yupin, it was his underling who replied again, his tone sneering.

'The place didn't look right without a little ash! By the lash, you people are always sure to tell us how lucky we are to have the ash geysers, how fertile our land can be! Guess what? Your forest is ash now, and it will grow back all the better afterwards! Just like our crops. You should thank us.'

He shifted slightly, revealing the weapon he was holding at his side. It was a coiled whip, but metal rather than leather. The entire length of it glowed red hot, ready to sear the skin of anything it touched. Maybe this was what had set the forest ablaze. Maybe practising with it was what had given the man that disturbing cut in his lip. She could see yellow teeth through the gash and had to look away. Sabira's mother held up her hands, palms up, showing that she was holding no weapon – her bow was still fastened to her back.

'This doesn't have to get ugly,' she said carefully.

Sabira could sense the tension. The taste of danger in the air was as heavy as the acrid smoke. She didn't understand why this was happening, but could feel it worsening by the second. Why were they doing this?

'We're not going to kill you,' Colonel Yupin said at last, unblinking. His words were soft and considered, and without a hint of compassion.

'We're not?' the sergeant major said, sounding surprised.

'Stay your hand, Sergeant Major Lifan. 'They can be useful, and tell the rest of their honourless people what they've seen.'

The colonel spat the words, and Sabira saw the hate in him. Not just hate for the three of them, but for everything they were, down to the blood and bone. Her mother's eyes narrowed and she said quietly to Yupin,

'Your mother was Aderasti. How can you do this to her people?'

How did she know this man? Sabira wondered. How Mother could even speak up to him, she didn't know, but her words went unanswered. Yupin's expression tightened, though he did not respond. Lifan – the man with the whip – reacted more strongly.

'Colonel, are we really just letting them go?' he demanded.

The sergeant major's leer sent another ripple of fear through Sabira, and even her mother lost some composure. She half turned, and Sabira thought she might grab her hand and pull them into a run – Kyran tensed, as if preparing to flee – but the colonel darted forward, quick as a cat, catching her arm.

'I didn't say they got to go without a scratch, Sergeant Major,' he said, looking into her eyes. His calmness set more dread in Sabira's belly than all of Lifan's threats.

'Let her go!' Kyran said, his voice hoarse with fear.

'Hold the children,' Yupin ordered a few of his men, and hard hands closed around Kyran's arms, pulling him from Sabira's grasp. Although a year Sabira's senior and fiercely brave, he hadn't yet reached a man's height. He struggled uselessly.

Other hands grabbed Sabira. 'Get off me!' she cried, though she couldn't move, let alone run, no matter how much she wanted to. They'd shoot her. They'd shoot her mother. The Ignatians closed in around them.

'Perhaps your daughter should get acquainted with the branding lash?' Lifan asked, leering at Taranna. 'She ought to learn some respect.'

He loosened his grip on his lash, allowing it to uncoil menacingly in his hand. Sabira's breath shortened, panic gripping her at the thought of sizzling metal touching her bare skin. This couldn't be real. It couldn't be happening.

'Leave them alone!' Taranna demanded. Lifan didn't bother to acknowledge her. 'Don't hurt my children!' she pleaded, turning to Yupin. 'They're not

21

even old enough to understand what this is about!'

And with a slow and awful kind of grace, the colonel held up a hand.

'Stand down, Lifan. They are not subject to our great laws,' he told the sergeant major. 'Not yet. One day, we will come to Adranna, and things will be different – yet you ought to remember, Sergeant Major, we are not animals. It is not their flesh that we desire, but their compliance.'

The sergeant major obeyed, but his eyes dragged over Sabira's body and she shivered, wishing she could hold her mother's hand.

'Teach the woman a lesson,' said Yupin, 'but don't break anything. She will need to be able to run afterwards. No need to touch the children – their fear will be enough.'

That fear took hold of Sabira with a bear's strength as soldiers grasped her mother. When the first full-fisted punch was thrown, Sabira screamed.

They didn't stop. First her mother's gut, then her face, then her side.

'Stop! Don't you dare hurt her!' Kyran cried, but no one cared to listen.

The thud of fists on flesh turned Sabira's legs to jelly. She screamed and screamed, but it earned her nothing except a stinging cuff from one of the men holding her. She fell silent.

'Understand,' said Colonel Yupin, 'this is of your

own making. There are consequences when your people wrong us. The rest will come soon enough.'

Sabira's mother cried out as she was again struck in the face. She fell, the men holding her letting it happen. It was easier to kick her when she was down. Sabira fought to get free, desperate to do something to help. She managed to pull an arm loose, but Yupin barked, 'Hold her,' and more arms obeyed.

'Don't struggle, it'll only make it worse,' someone whispered in Sabira's ear. She stopped, partly from shock. The voice was surprisingly young: a boy's voice in a soldier's body. She struggled for half a second more, managing to twist around for a moment, and caught a flash of his face before they caught hold of her once again. The boy looked as young as he had sounded – perhaps her brother's age – and seemed almost too thin to be carrying a musket, let alone holding Sabira prisoner. He had the goggles, though, just like the others. Without eyes, there was no pity to be seen, even if he had any.

'I'm sorry,' he went on, 'I've seen him do this before – but he's no liar. He'll let you go, as long as you don't fight him.' Another soldier growled at him to shut up, and she heard no more. Sabira was sure he was lying, but all she could do was watch as the men turned their black boots and gloves red with her mother's blood. Anger boiled through her veins and tears streaked her face. Surely they would kill her? She prayed to the mountain that they would stop at the next blow, or the next, before it was too late.

'Enough,' Yupin said, an eternity later. Instantly, the violence ceased. It was as if it had never begun, save for the evidence of her mother's battered form. 'Up,' he demanded, and Taranna was hauled to unsteady feet next to Sabira. The hands restraining her let go, and both were allowed to stand freely. But Colonel Yupin wasn't done.

'You have five seconds,' he stated, turning his back on Kyran, Sabira and their mother, as if he was bored. He watched the forest burn. 'Best make use of them. Count down, Sergeant Major Lifan.'

'Five!' the sergeant major yelled happily. Sabira stared, not understanding.

'Come on, Sabira,' Kyran said. He grabbed her hand and pulled, but she was numb, she couldn't move.

'Four!' he added, and the other Ignatians formed into a line, their muskets at attention. Sabira saw a flash of the boy soldier there, looking almost as afraid as she felt. Frozen, she turned wide, teary eyes to where her mother tottered, desperately hoping that she knew what to do.

'*Sabira!*' Kyran yelled, tugging at her arm. She staggered, unbalanced.

'Three!'

'Run,' Taranna mouthed through cut and bloody lips. The word sliced through Sabira's indecision. Her

24

muscles unstuck, and she ran, allowing Kyran to tug her into a sprint.

'Two!'

Nothing existed but Kyran's hand in hers, her legs hammering on the rocky path, back towards the foothills and the mountain path, towards home. Her feet pounded the hard, rocky ground, slipping and sliding in her desperation to escape.

'One!'

She was too frightened to think of anything except whether the next second would be her last.

'Fire!' Lifan's voice rang out over the landscape, echoing over the crackle and roar of the fire. Deafening cracks exploded behind her. Musket fire.

Kyran's hand was tugged from her own.

'Kyran!' she yelled, stopping and ducking to help him up. His face was ashen. She pulled his arm over her shoulder and tried to lift him to his feet. He staggered up with a cry of pain, and Sabira noticed the blood soaking his hunting trousers at the top of his leg.

She heard another runner coming up behind. She glanced over her shoulder: it was their mother, running awkwardly but alive.

Her face was a mass of blood and bruises and she was holding her arm tightly. Sabira could see red trickling from a gash beneath her fingers, and she realized with horror that her mother had been shot too. She stopped, looping Kyran's other arm around her own battered shoulders.

'Let's go,' she said, through gritted teeth.

They half dragged, half carried Kyran a few paces before the muskets fired a second time, the deafening cracks echoing through the valley. Sabira flinched, expecting to be hit – instead, laughter rang out from the Ignatians. What if they weren't quick enough to escape? What if the Ignatians changed their minds about letting them live? Kyran was sobbing, only half conscious.

'It'll be all right. We'll be all right,' Taranna reassured them both. 'We'll get you to Father, Kyran.' Sabira almost believed her, before another volley of musket fire cracked, and she flinched again.

'They're just trying to scare us,' her mother said, as they reached the mountain path. 'We're safe now.' But even though the musket salvos had stopped, and even as they put more distance between them and the Ignatians' laughter, it seemed to Sabira that nothing would ever feel safe again.

CHAPTER THREE

Six months later

Sabira was cleaning around her mother's skinning table, scrubbing the floor on her hands and knees. She could see Kyran inside, organizing their father's herb box with a thunderous frown on his face.

Sabira stole a glance at him as she dipped her brush in the bucket of soapy water, but dropped her eyes before he noticed her watching. She was avoiding talking to him. They always argued, these days – Kyran was much quicker to anger than he used to be, before the Ignatians had— She shook her head. She didn't like to think of what had happened in the forest. Couldn't.

Father and Uncle Mihnir were due home any day. They'd gone as part of a diplomatic delegation to Ignata. The Ignatian forest fire – and their treatment of Sabira's mother and brother – was just one symptom of how the relationship between the two countries was breaking down. Now, they were trying to fix it. The benefit of doing chores was being able to keep an eye out for her father and uncle's return. It helped that it was a mild summer's day, with a thin layer of meltwater glistening on the city's ice walls.

The delegation had been away since early spring, but it felt like for ever to Sabira. The whole family had been so proud when Father was selected. He hadn't expected the honour of the mission, but Sabira thought that perhaps *they*, his family, should have – he was the most well-respected healer in Adranna after all. It had been hard without his usual calming influence, though – especially with Uncle Mihnir gone too, accompanying the delegation as a packman – and it was a relief to know that he was on the way home.

She returned to her scrubbing, sighing.

'Sabira!'

In the road, as if from a dream, stood her father and Uncle Mihnir. Both carried large packs on their backs, and their clothes were dirtied by the long journey. Father looked tired from walking across nations, but his smile still drew Sabira. This was a man desperately glad to be home. Heart swelling, she dropped her scrubbing brush and ran to circle his waist with a hug. He laughed and tousled her hair, saying,

'I think you may have grown a whole hand.'

'That's what happens when you go away for ever,' Sabira mumbled into her father's chest. She hugged huge, bear-like Uncle Mihnir next.

'How's my favourite niece?' he boomed.

'I'm your only niece!' she replied, just before her uncle pulled his arms tight around her and lifted her off her feet until she squeaked and laughed.

She pulled herself free of the hug, and turned to her father. He held her at arm's length and said more seriously, 'How's Kyran? Keeping my medicines in order, I trust?'

She nodded. 'It's kept his mind off things,' she said quietly, so her brother wouldn't hear from inside. 'Some of the time, at least.'

Her father picked up the concern in her voice, his smile wavering as he turned to the house. The slate-roofed building was not large, but they had more than many. A room for her parents, one for her, one for Kyran and one for the whole family where meals were prepared and stories told over the fire pit. As was tradition, Sabira and her family had painted the uneven stone brick walls the same bright colours as Adranna's ice walls.

Beside the door were paintings daubed by the children in their early years – a hastily-drawn stick figure from Sabira and a bright blue, icicle-shaped frostsliver by Kyran. It was such a long time ago – Sabira felt like a different person now. Sabira grabbed her father's hand in one of hers and Uncle Mihnir's in the other, and dragged them to the little wooden door.

'Father and Uncle Mihnir are home!' she yelled as she pulled them inside.

Sabira's mother emerged from the back of the house, rushing to embrace her husband. Kyran set the box of herbs aside and stood up. He swayed for a moment, leaning on the wall to take the weight off his artificial leg.

The Ignatians stole his real one, Sabira thought with a flash of anger.

'Trust you to make it back hours after I sold the best of my hunt!' Mother said. 'We ought to be having a feast, not leftovers.'

'I'm sure Butcher Torran will be happy to return a cut or two,' said Sabira's father.

Kyran unpropped himself from the wall and said, 'I'll go. Can't have a celebration without good food.'

'Don't worry, Kyran,' Father said. 'I can get it.'

Kyran didn't take it as the courtesy it was.

'I may be broken, Father, but you don't have to treat me like it!' Kyran barked, and stomped for the door. 'I'll be back later,' he added, and left, shutting the door harder than was needed.

The family exchanged looks, but said nothing.

While Sabira's mother lit the fire, the three adults started to catch each other up on all the news. Hours passed, and Sabira assumed that Kyran had decided to take some time to cool off before returning. That wasn't unusual for him nowadays.

Eventually, tiring of waiting for the meat, they sat down to a feast of pastries and cheeses from the larder. The traditional feast meal of many courses, alternating spicy and plain, would have to wait – though Sabira was pleased to find that her father had brought back some Ignatian firefruit for dessert. They didn't get many sweet things on the mountain.

After they'd eaten, Sabira's eyelids began to droop. She intended to stay awake until Kyran got back, though, despite feeling so dozy. Where had he gone? she wondered. When her head bobbed low for the third time, Sabira forced herself to join the conversation in a bid to keep from nodding off.

'Did you manage to help in Ignata?' she asked her father. He paused before answering,

'You could say that. Things didn't go very well, but I gave what advice I could. Talks are ongoing; they plan to send a delegation of their own, come winter, so that's something, I suppose. Managed to heal a few people while I was there too. Plenty of work for healers in that place.'

'Is it so dangerous in Ignata?' Sabira asked, holding

out her little ash-cat. 'Do the ash-cats attack people?'

Sabira's father smiled at her fondly. 'Not often – but you'd be shocked at how many ailments those ash geysers of theirs cause – mostly lung problems,' her father replied. He turned to her mother, softening his voice. 'Oh, and speaking of problems, Taranna, I did see Yupin.'

Taranna's expression grew abruptly cold, and Sabira noticed how she lifted her fingers to the scar on her arm, where the musket ball had once lodged. Sabira shifted uncomfortably. The colonel featured in nearly all of her nightmares.

'Adranna is well shot of that family,' Taranna replied at last. 'The city welcomed them when his father married one of us, and how did his father repay us?'

'Was it the thieving, or the beatings, that they got him for in the end?' Mihnir asked.

'I think it was his trying to bribe that frost-cleric to send Yupin to the glacier,' said Sabira's father. 'They weren't going to choose him otherwise.'

'Either way, exile's too good for him,' Taranna said bitterly. Sabira stayed silent. She had the feeling that they'd forgotten she was listening – and she was curious.

'Well, we've seen he's now an officer in the Ignatian army, and I think he's been sharing his ideas with his new people.'

'What do you mean, Rabten?' asked Taranna.

'Their demands. They wanted a hundred frost-slivers,' said Sabira's father. 'Can you imagine? The idea of them being sold at market . . . it's just wrong.'

'They don't know the glacier like we do,' her mother said. 'They think the frostslivers are a tool that they don't have. It's no surprise to hear someone say that they want what you've got. Some people will pay anything to get even.' Taranna paused, apparently thinking on what she had just said, and then added, 'What exactly were they going to pay in anyway?'

'Muskets,' her husband replied in a flat tone.

Taranna's eyes narrowed. 'Weapons? They wanted to buy sacred allies with weapons?'

'It was suggested that they could be hunting aids.'

Rabten said it with so little emotion that Sabira barely recognized her father in his voice. Her mother had the opposite reaction. Already angry, what she'd heard made Taranna leap to her feet, almost knocking over her chair.

'Muskets! Skill-less noise-makers to frighten off most every animal on the mountain, and bring down snow slides on the rest!' Taranna cried in outrage.

Muskets: the weapons that destroyed my brother's life, thought Sabira. But although the thought hung in the air, nobody spoke it.

Sabira didn't know whether her parents were really angry at each other or just at the world in general, but she found she didn't want to listen any more. She padded outside as quickly as possible, where the meaning of the voices did not carry. Finding a spot on the doorstep to sit, Sabira took a breath of the early evening air. The chill was a refreshing change from the close, smoky room.

She pulled the ash-cat toy from her pocket, and began to play with its now rather battered paws, trying to calm down.

After barely a minute, footsteps came echoing through the half dark. Sabira recognized the familiar clunking gait. Kyran. Sabira waved to her brother until he looked up, breaking a seemingly intense train of thought. Slowly, he made his way over to her.

Under his trouser lay a hinged leg assembly of wood and metal pins designed by her father. It was much better than the simple pegs that she had seen some patients managing with, but it was no substitute for the real thing.

Kyran stopped in front of her, slightly out of breath and holding a small waxed paper package from the butcher. He'd left his cane again; it was propped next to the doorway beside her, useless as always. He always pretended to forget it, though Sabira was certain he just had too much pride to use it. She wished he would look after himself better.

'You get some good cuts?' Sabira asked, looking at the package.

Her brother laughed coldly. 'Not likely. Barely

anything better than average left. You know that the frost-clerics get first pick? Don't see what they've done to earn that.' Bitterness dripped from his words.

'They just do what they've always done,' Sabira said.

He handed over the small parcel of meat that he had been sent for. 'They'll see their mistake one day. I'll make sure of it.'

Sabira heard the confidence in his voice. Did he think they'd allow him to walk the bonding path, even though he'd missed his chance? They never took people after their assigned day on the bonding path had come and gone. It wasn't fair, but Sabira didn't think that made any difference.

'I think . . . I think maybe they won't ever change their minds, Kyran,' she said gently.

'You think so now, little ash-cat, but . . .' he replied, smiling and leaning in, as if whispering a secret. He looked both ways and added more quietly, 'I'm going myself. They don't get to decide I'm not worthy because . . . because of this.' He nodded down at his leg in disgust.

'I don't think your leg being like this is what made them say—' Sabira began, but her brother cut her off.

'I don't need their approval. I can do it on my own.'

Sabira felt her stomach twist in fear. She believed both that he meant it, and that it was possible. If anyone could climb the mountain alone with a false leg, Kyran could – but he shouldn't.

'I don't want you to die!' she blurted.

Sabira knew how dangerous the path could be, particularly without a guide. Even healthy people didn't come back sometimes. Kyran ignored her, muttering, 'I've been thinking this through for a while. I'm sure I know how to get past the guards to the path, and once I'm on the stairs no one is going to stop me. Well, we'll see soon enough.'

It was only then that Sabira noticed the full bag strapped to her brother's back, and her worry began to turn to terror. Not only was he going; he intended to leave now. Her breath quickened, sending fog out into the icy air. She was suddenly sure that this conversation was important. The kind she'd remember her whole life.

'You don't have to do this,' she said, trying to keep her voice in check. 'It's terrible what happened, but you could still be happy, I know you could. Father would like you to be a healer too one day. Isn't that a good life?'

Kyran's gaze was fixed on the ground.

'What if you don't come back?' she pleaded. 'Mother and Father . . . and me . . . you can't leave us!'

For a moment, she thought she had reached him, but when he raised his eyes, she saw the resolution there. Sabira didn't know what else she could say to sway him. Dread built in the pit of her stomach and it got worse as he spoke, etching his intentions into the air.

'I'm sorry things haven't been how they should be. When I've got my frostsliver, things will be different, you'll see. I'll be complete again – maybe it can form me a whole new leg!'

'Please, Kyran, please don't go,' she begged.

'I wanted Father to come back before I went. In case something went wrong. Now he's here. You'll be all right. I'll see everyone soon.'

Sabira felt panic rising in her. What could she do? Should she call to their parents? They could restrain him for now, but Kyran would never forgive her – and nobody could really stop him in the long run if his mind was made up. There was no time to think.

'You can't—'

'I'm going, Sabira,' he said, cutting her off. 'And you'd better not tell Mother and Father. Not before it's too late for them to do anything. Promise me.'

Sabira's breath caught in her throat – but she nodded. If she told them now, he would only make plans to leave another time. He had made his choice. 'Take this with you, at least,' she said, grabbing the cane from beside the door and offering it to her brother. He stared at it, and Sabira added hastily, 'Lots of people use a stick when on a journey, not just people with injuries.'

Perhaps it was the pleading expression on her face, or maybe Kyran saw some wisdom in safety, because after a moment he did take it.

'And . . . and . . . take this too,' she added, holding out her ash-cat figurine. 'For luck.'

'But I made it for you,' Kyran said gently.

'And I love it more than anything. That's why I want you to have it,' Sabira insisted, pressing it into his hand.

'All right. Thank you.' He accepted the gift gravely and started to turn away from her. But before he could leave, she stood on her tiptoes and wrapped her arms around his shoulders.

'Don't. . .' she tried to say, though it came out in a squeak. Sabira wasn't even sure if Kyran had heard her. He pulled away and started to walk into the night. Sabira watched and watched, tears filling her eyes.

'See you soon, little ash-cat!' he said without looking back.

Sabira stayed there, frozen on the brink of tears as he strode towards the city wall, heading for the base of the bonding path. He turned a corner, waving over his shoulder. Before she knew it, Kyran was gone. Gone to meet his fate on the bonding path. Gone to touch the glacier and take his piece of it, or else be defeated by the mountain.

Sabira sat on the steps, and put her head in her hands.

CHAPTER FOUR

Six months later

This time last year, Kyran had been alive and well. He had gifted Sabira the ash-cat and been chosen for the honour of bonding a frostsliver. He'd been so happy. Sabira's world had been strong and stable and complete. Now, everything had fallen apart.

It was six months since Kyran had left her behind and hobbled up the bonding path, leaning on the cane that she had begged him to use, carrying the ash-cat in his pocket.

They hadn't found a body – but then, they rarely did.

The shame of it hadn't left her. She should've stopped him. He was a head taller, but she still should've tried. She should've run to her parents the moment he told her his plan, ignoring the promise she had made him. She had been so stupid. Aderast didn't care how strong his courage and will were. Why had she thought that they could be enough?

She stood beside her mother outside the temple, set into the mountain a little above the city. There was only one red ribbon on her mother's arm now, for her one remaining child. It was a constant reminder that cut Sabira every time she saw it. She watched as Ignatians snaked their way up the narrow, winding path towards the waiting city council, along with her father. She could almost feel the prickle of heat, the memory of that day in the burning forest, and shuddered in sudden fear.

'Vermin,' her mother spat, her eyes narrowed. This was supposed to be a diplomatic delegation – but open the gates to evil, her mother had said, and you shouldn't be surprised to find a knife at your throat.

'At school they say that there are a thousand men at the bottom of the mountain,' Sabira said, hoping to be told it wasn't true.

'A show of force,' her mother confirmed.

A demonstration of what a siege would look like, Sabira realized. The Ignatians knew that Adranna wouldn't survive without trade from other mountain villages, and even other nations.

'Is there going to be a war?' she found herself asking.

'Your father says the Ignatian High Tribunal won't be willing to take that kind of risk,' her mother reassured her. 'The plains nations are already wary of their neighbour. If we were attacked, it might tip them over into openly opposing Ignata. Try not to worry.'

Sabira did her best. No enemy had seen inside the walls of the city since they were built at the order of the First Bonded, the legendary founder of Adranna. The only route to the city was steep and narrow, easy to defend. And yet the city council had seen fit to invite the Ignatians into its sanctuary.

'Come on,' said her mother, drawing Sabira aside. 'I don't want to watch this. Besides, you're going to be late.'

As she followed her mother past the crowds outside the temple and up the narrow path to the shrine, Sabira had the strange sensation of catching up with Kyran, stepping into his shoes. Every night, her dreams were tinged with the blue light of the glacier, the light of magic, the flame with no heat: frostfire. Today she would learn whether those dreams could ever be real, when the frost-cleric chose her, or didn't. Sabira wasn't sure how much it mattered any more.

As disturbing as the Ignatian presence was, worries

about her own future made their way to the front of her mind. A frostsliver would be a great honour. It would also be a burden, one of responsibility and expectation. Did she want that? She had thought so once. Before the burning forest. Before Kyran. Now, she just felt afraid.

She arrived at the shrine with every part of her wanting to bolt or hide. Her mother hugged her briskly and promised to fetch Father and wait for her outside the temple, once the day's diplomacy was finished. Sabira sat in the small waiting room with the others who had come of age this year, her heart racing.

Hours later, having watched a dozen other potential bonded enter and leave the testing room, often in tears, she felt even more nervous.

Why did she have to be last? The wait was agonizing.

The testing room door opened and Sabira almost leapt out of her chair as the frost-cleric who would decide Sabira's worthiness walked in. The blue glow of frostfire showed at her neckline, marking her out as special, as if her flowing scarlet robes were not enough. Sabira watched the woman with something akin to awe. She seemed so poised, so sure of herself in her role. Would Sabira wear robes like that one day? Would she be a teacher, an advisor, a spiritual leader like her? Too many paths, and none of them called to her – not yet anyway.

She was given no time to guess, as the last person to

be tested ran out from behind the woman and made straight for the exit, slamming the door behind him without looking back. Sabira guessed from the half-supressed sob that he had not been chosen either. She gulped.

The cleric fixed her gaze on Sabira and quickly stalked across the room, shoes echoing on the smooth stone, speaking over the rhythm.

'I am Tserah. I will be conducting your Choosing.'

Sabira gripped the arms of her chair, her anxiety getting to her – Tserah was known to be a strict teacher.

'I know of you, Sabira,' she said levelly. 'You've been through a lot these last years.'

Sabira's fingers tightened on the wooden armrests. 'Will that count against me?'

'Not directly,' said the frost-cleric. 'This way, please.'

Sabira followed Tserah into the testing room and closed the door. It was only a few paces across, and had no furniture. There were two cushioned areas for seating, one next to a grilled window at the rear that the frost-cleric settled on to, cross-legged. The other was surrounded by red candles and sticks of incense emitting heady fumes.

Nervously, Sabira copied the frost-cleric's pose, and breathed deeply. Immediately she felt light-headed, the smoke clouding her mind. She noted that over by the window, Tserah had much clearer air. Maybe this was part of the test.

'All you need do is talk,' Tserah said. 'I will show you things, and you will talk a little about them. I may ask questions. Nothing too complicated. Are you ready?'

Sabira quivered in her place, too nervous even to nod. Tserah's face softened.

'You know the tale of Adranna's founder, the First Bonded?' she asked, speaking in a calming tone. 'Well, when they walked down deep into the mountain and cut the first frostsliver right from the very source of the glacier, they had no idea of the danger they were in. The bonding could have killed them, if they'd had the wrong kind of mind for it. The First Bonded was lucky to be a good match. This discussion will simply tell you whether you could be too. There's no need to worry about failing – not being chosen is not a failure, just a different path.'

This helped Sabira's nerves a little, though perhaps that was only because her head was beginning to swim in the room's close air. She nodded, not knowing what else to do.

'All right, then. We shall begin,' said Tserah. She placed her hand on the glowing frostsliver at her neck. The ice quivered, turning to a thick liquid, burning with frostfire as the frostsliver flowed out on to the palm of her hand.

Sabira had seen frostslivers several times during her lessons at the temple. Some of the frost-clerics kept them hidden beneath their robes, but others were less reverent. Some even used the magic of their bonded partners to help teach. Each time the frostslivers' wondrous, transformative powers had amazed Sabira – but today she was far too anxious to feel a sense of awe.

The piece of living ice slithered into a glowing blue shape upon Tserah's palm – a thick vertical line attached to a thin circle. Sabira guessed what it had to mean.

'Does that represent a frostsliver?' she questioned.

'You tell me,' Tserah said, giving nothing away.

It was a simple start, but Sabira froze for a moment. Her mind hadn't quite registered that the test had begun, and she was unsure of what was expected. That incense. She couldn't think right. Tserah opened a small leather-bound book, resting it in her lap. As Sabira spoke, she began writing in it with a charcoal stick.

'It's what I'm here for,' Sabira quickly stammered. Ridiculous – the cleric knew that already. 'It will change me . . . if you choose me, I mean.'

This wasn't going very well.

'The mountain provides them, and we join with them – I just wish I knew why it did. It only seems to be causing us trouble lately.'

Should she have said that? The frost-cleric was still writing. Sabira decided to wait, rather than talk herself into any more trouble.

When Tserah had finished writing, her frostsliver morphed once again, becoming a wide, upwards-pointing arrow, a triangle with no base.

'Aderast. Home,' Sabira replied instantly. 'The place where we all ought to be safe.'

Sabira stopped and considered, fighting the confusion that had settled into her brain. That was Adranna the city, not Aderast the mountain.

'It'll always be a fight with the mountain to keep that, though. We have to respect it, remember how easily it can change our fortunes.'

'You talk about the mountain as if it has desires, and has the will to act on them.'

'Doesn't it?' Sabira asked, genuinely unsure, and saw Tserah scribble another note.

More and more symbols and shapes followed, and Sabira did her best to discuss them, not knowing if anything she said was right. Her head kept getting fuzzier, and under the gentle questioning, she felt like her interview was taking a long time. Was that good or bad?

She sensed her words grow looser as they went on, being more honest than she really wanted to be. There didn't seem to be any obvious wrong answers – there was no mathematics, or spelling tests, or anything like that. Instead, they spoke of her family, of her life experiences, of her hopes and fears. It was more like Tserah was judging her as a person, weighing her responses and calculating who Sabira really was.

'All right, we're done,' Tserah said, after what felt like for ever. Sabira's heart sank. She was sure she'd failed. She was glad of the incense numbing her thoughts – maybe that was what it was truly for. 'You'll want to take some time to say goodbye to your family before you leave in a few days' time,' Tserah added, standing with deliberate grace. Sabira didn't understand. It didn't make any sense that she would need to do anything but go and apologize to her parents for letting them down. Then the meaning pried its way in.

'I . . . You want me . . .' she said dumbly.

'You have been chosen to bond a frostsliver, Sabira,' the frost-cleric clarified. Something between joy and abject terror erupted in Sabira's belly, an entire world of possibilities opening up. She wasn't prepared for this – couldn't really believe it.

Why had she been chosen? She was no better than anyone else. And surely she had failed too often to deserve a frostsliver? Not just in the test, but generally.

'There must be others . . .' Sabira said, not knowing quite why she was protesting.

'And there will be. Aderast knows we may need every frostsliver, if events continue to go badly.'

Was that why she had been allowed to pass? The city needed extra defenders? She knew the magic could be used to fight, if it came to it.

'Are there . . . are there not enough?' Sabira said,

voice shaking.

Tserah's voice grew firm.

'We choose people on their merits. Aderast would accept nothing else. Now, stand up.'

She shepherded Sabira into the shrine's waiting room, away from the red ritual candles and the incense and said, 'Return to me here when you are ready. You will not need to bring anything but your body, mind and resolve.'

Sabira only managed to stand and stare, still bewildered.

Tserah smiled. 'Cheer up – there's enough unhappiness with those who *don't* get chosen. Oh, and you'll want to get as much fresh air as you can. That incense may be pleasant enough when loosening the tongue, but it can sting a little afterwards when you're not used to it.'

Sabira did her best to arrange her face into something more appreciative, and then charged from the shrine before the spell over it could break. She shut the heavy door, breathing hard, unsure what to feel. It seemed at any moment Tserah's voice might call her back to tell her that there had been a mistake, but long seconds passed and nothing changed.

Outside, the air was crisp and new, the early evening already turning the sky a vivid shade of violet. Sabira felt new too, her head clearing as she breathed in deeply. She walked slowly towards where her mother and father waited for her outside the temple – now empty of the crowds that had gathered earlier. They watched Sabira anxiously as she descended from the shrine.

'She said yes,' Sabira told them as she drew near, preferring not to keep them in suspense. It felt like she was making it up. Her father grinned and congratulated her warmly, and her mother put a hand to her mouth, covering sudden emotion. Her shining eyes said it all: the joy, and the fear of her daughter venturing on to the mountain.

'I'll be safe, Mother,' she reassured her. 'They'll take care of me. It's afterwards that I'm worried about. I don't know if I'm cut out to be a frost-cleric.'

At that, Taranna bent to hug her daughter as if it was the last time she would get the chance. It might have been embarrassing in other circumstances, though Sabira was too glad to care – her mother rarely showed this much emotion. Her mother began to gush advice in a voice that sounded like it was holding back tears. Tears that could have been of joy, or sadness, or both.

'Being a frost-cleric isn't the only option,' she said, 'They may all have frostslivers, but lots of other important people do too, even those who don't need their magic. They're great advisors, and that's often more important than their power. Almost all of the city council have them. So does the chief librarian. Your father was offered one when he was younger.'

Sabira looked at her mother in surprise. Her eyes then flicked to her father, who looked almost embarrassed by the revelation. He tried to hide it by saying kindly, 'You could always refuse too, if you wanted.'

Sabira hadn't even known that refusing was allowed. It might be easier. There would be no particular expectations of her without the frostsliver. Down the other path lay danger, the unknown – and her brother's lost desire.

'No, I can't refuse,' Sabira said quietly. 'Kyran would never forgive me.'

Her father's smile faded a little at the mention of his son, but he told her, 'Your brother isn't here – you don't have to fight his battle for him.'

Sabira thought about it. Was this something that she was doing as some kind of penance, some way of making up for her past mistakes? She hoped not. Kyran had wanted the frostsliver to prove that he could get it, but that was not what was in Sabira's heart. Yes, she would like to think that he would be proud of her, but this meant something else to her too. She wanted her life to make some kind of difference.

'I'm not doing it for him,' she realized aloud. 'I'm going to do this for me . . . even if I don't completely know why yet.'

Sabira knew as she spoke the words that they were true. She was still unsure, but it no longer felt like a weight to be dragged. A small smile made its way on to her features as she looked between her parents' faces, wanting them to believe in her decision. Each of them reached out a hand for one of her shoulders, and Sabira felt her chest swell, grateful for their understanding.

'Maybe, with your frostsliver, the way forward will be clearer,' her father offered.

It didn't seem likely, but Sabira was ready to accept that. The future would come, no matter what she did, and change was not always bad. She nodded, looking back to Aderast's great heights. To claim her frostsliver, she'd have to walk the bonding path to the glacier, and cut her piece of it. Sabira tried not to let the thought overwhelm her, but she couldn't help but stare upwards to where fate would take her in just a few short days. The stairs of the bonding path looked like they wound on to infinity.

'You'll not want to dally up there,' her mother suggested. 'You can't get caught out in the open overnight that high on the mountainside.'

Her mother didn't add that it could prove fatal. She didn't have to – it was already on Sabira's mind.

Nothing else would matter until Aderast gave her its bounty, or took her into its embrace.

But Sabira wasn't going to let the mountain

intimidate her.

Something caught her eye below, a procession moving through the city streets, towards Adranna's main gate. Black-clothed people, marching in a column. The Ignatians. Sabira felt her stomach turn. They were supposed to be staying for months – they couldn't be leaving already, could they?

'What's wrong?' she demanded.

Her father tried to calm her, saying, 'It's nothing for you to worry about, Sabira. You should stay focused on—'

'Please, Father. Tell me.'

He looked at her mother, who nodded.

'The talks . . . they haven't gone well. Meihu, the judge leading the Ignation delegation had some promising things to say about improved ties, trade and so on. Then Colonel Yupin pushed in. Gave a speech – more of a rant – about how we Aderasti will never change our ways, and people like his mother paid the price. She got some ash-related illness years back and died. He blamed us, and things went downhill from there.'

'You mean . . . ?' Sabira questioned.

'It's fallen apart,' he admitted. 'The delegation is leaving to deliver the news to Ignata. I . . . I don't know what we're going to do next.'

Sabira gulped, thinking on what that might mean. She looked up at Aderast, worry eating at her once more. It made her all the more nervous to know that her father didn't have the answers, that he didn't know what the future might bring.

And despite the chance she'd just been given, neither did she.

PART II

CHAPTER FIVE

Sabira followed the winding staircase towards the glacier, glancing nervously back to where she knew Mihnir and Tserah were waiting on the bonding path – but they'd already been swallowed up by the curve of the mountain.

She carried on down. It felt as if she was walking into a painted landscape, every brushstroke becoming more detailed with each nervous step. The wind had dropped, thank the mountain, and the fog had started to clear. Deeper into the valley she went, losing sight of the other Aderasti peaks. Soon, she came to the last string of red prayer flags and the last section of stairs.

Here, the stone steps were slippery underfoot. Even with her arms held out for balance, the path was treacherous and the wind threatened to tear back her hood and whip out her long, raven hair. About halfway down, Sabira felt the ground slide from under her feet and she hit the steps awkwardly, the impact sending a jolt of pain up her side.

Tears stung her eyes. If she'd been younger, she might've let them fall – but she was fourteen now, almost a woman grown. Sabira pulled herself up, ignored her new bruises, and continued until she met the edge of the glacier as it ground past the shore. Up close, the river of ice was even more impressive, its pristine surface casting its pale, otherworldly blue frostfire. As she watched it slide down the mountain, Sabira noticed a number of pits and crevasses dotting the glacier's surface. She'd have to tread carefully as she searched for her frostsliver.

Steeling herself, Sabira stepped on to the glacier. She almost overbalanced as it began to carry her away, but after a wobble she set off across the icy expanse to find her companion for life, her own small sliver of Aderast. *If it accepts me*, she thought darkly.

She had to be careful – touching the glacier with exposed skin could be deadly. The frost-clerics chose their candidates carefully, but even so the bonding didn't always take. She remembered the whispered words of Kyran's stories: *The bonding can kill, or maim, or make something monstrous.*

Sabira very much wanted to prove her brother wrong, but it was all too true that some disappeared on their bonding journey, never to be seen again. That was hardly surprising: crevasses pitted the glacier's surface, and the weather this high up was always a threat. Instead of worrying about the bonding itself, she thought, she ought to keep her wits about her, no matter how much reason they had to stray.

Some distance on to the glacier, Sabira felt the time was right. She crouched down to begin her work. Kneeling on the solid river sent a chill sneaking through her thick trousers and into her blood. Even an Aderasti was not immune to the cold. She had to fight off shivers as she finished retrieving her cutting tool from its sheath – she was going to need steady hands.

Sabira brushed off a patch of ice that looked relatively smooth, and readied the tiny metal coring tube. She held it over the ice, hesitating.

There would be no going back from this.

If she did it, she would have to make decisions about her future, big ones, and there would be a second voice in her head – her frostsliver. Things would be expected of her. She would have responsibility – and maybe even a little power.

The empty necklace that would soon hold the frostsliver suddenly felt heavy around her neck. She could still go back, say that the bonding had not worked. The thought wormed into her, comforting, easy.

No. She felt a need, deep inside, to succeed where others had not. Despite the danger, Sabira wanted this.

She put the coring tool to ice, and began turning its handle.

Its bladed teeth bit in, showering up powder. Sabira was half afraid that the glacier would open and swallow her whole. Instead, it simply carried her slowly downhill to the tune of cracking ice.

As the cylinder sank deeper, the ice made a slight ring, like a finger on thin glass, barely resisting at all. It was almost like it wanted to be freed. Like it knew what Sabira was going to ask of it.

Nearly done, she thought, as the corer screwed down to its base. The glacier's hold weakened, and Sabira began to work the cut ice back and forth until she heard a snap. She pulled the ice reverently from its hole, dropped it into her hand and laid down the tool.

A hand-span in length, the thin cylinder of ice was a cold weight on her gloved palm. The end tapered slightly where it had been snapped off, making it look a little like an icicle, and tiny flecks of frostfire danced inside. The sides were so smooth, so even – far better than her halting technique should have produced. It was perfect, and it was hers.

She could almost sense its mind on the edge of her thoughts, like a chorus of crystal voices.

Sabira was sorely tempted to pull off a glove and touch it, to begin the bonding immediately, but she had to get to safe ground first. She stood, and saw that the glacier had carried her further than she had expected. It would take her a little while to navigate her way back. It didn't matter. Having the frostsliver with her, even un-bonded, made her heart sing with success.

'See you soon,' she whispered to her family, somewhere down below.

A deafening bang sounded from above, and she almost dropped her frostsliver. A rumble followed, vibrating through the glacier so strongly that Sabira felt it shuddering under her boots.

She snapped her gaze up to the mountain peak, and felt her face drain of blood. The snow further up was sweeping rapidly down the mountainside in a torrent of searing cold death, heading directly towards the glacier.

The end of the world was coming. Armageddon in white.

For a long, stupid moment, she froze, staring up in horror. Then Sabira felt the weight of the thin cylinder in her glove, and resolve beat in her chest. Shelter, she needed shelter. She glanced around desperately.

Close by, she saw an ice outcropping several times her height and set off for it at a run, the rumble of the avalanche growing. She didn't have long. Ten seconds? Twenty?

Sabira skidded on the ice and her legs came out from under her. She tumbled awkwardly, landing flat on her stomach. The force of it drove the wind from her lungs, but worse, it made her fingers loosen their grip.

The precious frostsliver shot from her hand and skipped across the glacier surface. Time slowed. End over end it bounced, far out of Sabira's reach until it spun to a halt, lodged in the ice and melted away, claimed back by the glacier. Her chance had been stolen.

She screamed, but forced herself to stagger to her feet and run. The roar of the avalanche chased her and her boots continued to slide as she hurtled towards the outcropping. She skidded to a halt, realizing too late that there was no ground under it, just a deep, dark pit.

She fell, spinning as she tried for some kind of footing. Her gloves scrabbled for purchase on the slippery surface. She managed to jam her feet between cracks and find something resembling handholds. She clung to the ice as the mountain's roar swelled and the world fell on her.

Everything went white, and the thunder of rolling snow blotted out her hearing. The avalanche's blasting power was deflected by her protective ice wall, but plenty of it got around and under, buffeting at Sabira where she hung on, flowing into the crack below her in great drifts.

Every hellish second was a lifetime filled with bludgeoning impacts. It felt like the mountain was trying to throw her off. She was slipping.

Her left foot tore from its position, and then the right, leaving her dangling by the slightest of holds. Sabira clung on with every bit of strength she had, but it was a losing battle.

You can't fight the mountain.

The ice snapped under her glove, and suddenly nothing was holding her. Sabira dropped into the crevasse, a torrent of snow pursuing her. It drenched her, enveloping her in its freezing, choking embrace.

CHAPTER SIX

Claws of pain woke Sabira, a steady stabbing pain in her knee. She had only felt such a searing ache once before, when she had fractured her arm playing on Adranna's walls. Then, her parents had been there to take care of her. Now there was no one.

Blue light surrounded her, frostfire glowing through the snow. The snow itself was pressed in close, packed in all around her, paralysing, suffocating. Disorientated, it took Sabira a moment to recognize where she was – under the avalanche, completely buried in white.

Instinctively, Sabira had stretched her arms up as she fell and inflated her lungs as far as they would go – that was what you were supposed to do in an avalanche. It had bought her time, but not much.

Her first impulse now was to panic, to thrash and scream in a futile attempt to break free. She was going to die down here, trapped and immobile under the glacier's soft light, frozen like some kind of morbid statue. *No, no, no. Not like this.*

Sabira closed her eyes and forced herself to be calm. Heavy breathing would only kill her quicker. In and out. Slow it down. In. Out.

Her head throbbed, and Sabira guessed that, like her knee, she had knocked it on something on the way down.

It could have been worse. She could have split her head open on the ice. Not dead yet. Not yet.

Sabira wiggled her right arm, the one closest to her face, trying to shift the snow. To her great relief, it moved. The snow wasn't densely packed enough to lock her in place, thank the mountain.

Her fingers worked and wriggled until she had made a larger area around her mouth to breathe in – but her air was already growing stale. No panic. No time to panic.

Sabira knew how dangerous it would be to try and dig herself out – she could collapse the rest of the avalanche on her, or exhaust her air twice as fast. But staying put meant death, so what choice did she have?

The crevasse must have been partially filled by the avalanche before she fell, or there would be nothing left of her but a smear at the bottom. She couldn't be too far down, or she wouldn't have lived through the fall. It was even possible that she was close to the surface.

She pushed through the fear and, first one limb and then another, slowly began to wrestle her way upwards. Her knee hurt too much to put weight on it, so she worked with only her arms and other leg. Every motion brought more snow down on her, the stuff trying to get into her eyes, her nose, her mouth. It was slow, so slow, and taking even a gasp of breath was hard.

Horror stories crept into her head, tales of people who were trapped thinking they were the right way up, actually digging downwards. Digging their own graves. Before the terrible idea could sink in, she felt the snow in front of her give way, and her upper body flopped through sideways. Gulping in air, she rolled over to look up, a twinge of relief fighting the rest of her emotions. Above, between banks of snow, she saw the lip of the crevasse. Thank the mountain, there wasn't that far to the surface.

Still, the creaking and grinding of the glacier reminded Sabira that with every moment, it was carrying her further down the mountain, away from Tserah,

Mihnir and the bonding path – and home. She listened to her instincts, hobbling to her feet. As she rested weight on her injured leg, her knee twinged painfully. Maybe a torn ligament? That was something she'd seen her father diagnose before. It was the kind of thing that could be permanent, if untreated. Though that would only matter if she could get out of here, so she limped to the wall of the crevasse and heaved herself up on to the first available ledge.

The experience was agony, and if it weren't for the cold numbing her leg, she didn't think she could have done it. She remembered Kyran, his maimed leg, his screams of pain from her father's surgery. He had survived worse than this. The thought of her brother pushed her on. What would he have done, if this had happened to him? *Had* it happened to him? Sabira decided that she didn't want to know.

Under the frostfire, time stayed frozen in a perpetual twilight. Sabira had no idea how many hours she spent bathed by it as she grew closer to the surface, alternating between painful climbing and slow careful crawls along ledges. She was more tired than she had ever been. Her limbs ached, and she hadn't eaten since before they'd set out that morning.

Finally, she grasped the lip of the hole. Pushing through the pain, Sabira used everything she had, including her injured leg, to propel her up and on to flat ground.

She flopped flat on her back upon the snow-covered glacier, chest heaving, knee throbbing, vision blurred with pain and exhaustion. It was done. She had made it.

Except she wasn't done. Still there was more to overcome, for as she blinked at the sudden light, Sabira saw exactly where she was.

Alone in an alien landscape.

CHAPTER SEVEN

The world had changed while Sabira was below. Before, the dark crags of the mountain had jutted all around, but there was little trace of them now. The landscape was a uniform white and its contours were rounded off, like a giant carpenter had planed off all the edges. Every small landmark she remembered from before was buried. Long, straight tears in the snow showed where the moving glacier ended and the banks of the mountain began.

Her relief at escaping her living burial quickly faded – it had been only the first step.

Survival depended on her staying in control, and

being rational. No emotion, she told herself, though she felt overwhelmed with fear. She couldn't help picturing her parents' faces as they learnt the mountain had come for their other child too.

Sabira shut her eyes, breathed, opened them again. She stood up unsteadily. She had to find her way back to the steps, to Mihnir and Tserah. She hoped they were safe. The avalanche had been large enough to swamp the valley, even high up where they had been waiting for Sabira, and that meant— No, she shook the thought away. All she had to do was stay close to the moving edge of the glacier and follow it back uphill.

Sabira limped for the nearest bank. Her knee was greater agony with each dragged step but she tried to ignore it, and when she reached the edge of the glacier, she tumbled off into the drift beyond.

Sabira rested for a moment, allowing the cold to numb her leg a little. She gazed out on the snowy calm. How had this happened? These days, experienced climbers periodically climbed the mountain and triggered small, controlled snow slides. It was meant to stop more dangerous avalanches from building up. She shook her head. Right now that wasn't important; she had to concentrate on finding the others.

She levered herself up, and started to climb the slope. The weather had cleared, and Sabira would have found the scene beautiful under other circumstances, with the gentle hills of white flowing past her upon the glacier, and the sky a hard, brilliant blue. Instead, it felt like she was the only one left in the world, limping along with only pain for company.

The glacier creaked and groaned at her under its snowy burden, and Sabira chose to believe it was encouraging her rather than taunting. As she trudged along, the wind picked up and blew flecks of light snow directly into her face. She narrowed her eyes and pulled her hood down tight.

'Keep going,' she whispered to herself, then repeated it as a slow mantra.

But it didn't stop her mind from racing. What if she really was alone up here? What if she made her injury so bad that it never healed properly? What if she never saw her family again? Had Kyran felt like this? The questions flew past in her head and then twisted around to cycle again.

Eventually, when her worries had scored grooves in her mind and her limbs felt like lead, the wind began to change. Sabira raised her head and saw that she was almost back to the steps. They had been buffeted in her absence, the base disappearing under the blanket of white, but the rest looked clear enough to ascend. She looked towards the ridgeline anxiously.

It was as she'd feared: even up there, Tserah and

Mihnir would have been exposed to the force of the avalanche.

Sabira didn't want to think about it. Losing her uncle would be bad enough on its own, but without him and Tserah, she didn't know whether she could make it down the mountain. Uncle Mihnir had all the supplies and emergency equipment – without that, she was done for. She swallowed and hobbled faster.

Sabira approached the snow-buried foot of the steps. It was worryingly quiet. Her blood thudded faster in her ears as she stared up, searching, searching and searching with every pain-filled stumble. 'Mihnir! Tserah!' she called, once, twice. Again and again.

There was no one standing on those steps, though. Not at the base, nor further up. Sabira knew what that meant – there was no escaping it. They were gone, and soon Sabira would be too.

She wanted to cry, but tears didn't come. Instead, she kept on shuffling forward. Her fate didn't feel real. There was no great event to mark her end. It was almost as if it was happening to someone else. The realization was coming, climbing up her spine. Soon she would break down and give in.

As the despair swelled, Sabira took one last look over the place that was going to claim her. She was close enough to see detail in the hillside now, not that it mattered. Except, something attracted her attention – a flicker high up at the valley top.

It was just a small thing, barely more than a glint of light. The glint of frostfire. The glint of Tserah's frost-sliver.

They were alive.

CHAPTER EIGHT

One last step, she thought, and slid herself up with a stab of pain.

Sabira had finally climbed to where she had left Mihnir and Tserah several hours earlier, working her way to the place where she'd seen the blue light. The wind was bitter. Sabira defended her eyes with her arm, her back to the glacier as she looked down the mountainside path towards home.

Except there was no path.

The steps that had guided Sabira up from Adranna were gone, torn away from the mountainside.

The weight of the snow had been too much for the

ancient carved steps, and the rock had sheared. What was left was slick, smooth and impassable. They were cut off from Adranna.

Sabira's mind spun.

Climbing teams with every tool at their disposal might be able to manage it, but Sabira couldn't. That rock wall was like a sheet of ice, with barely a hand-hold. The few there were crumbled and spat pebbles even as Sabira watched; the whole area was unstable.

She turned towards the faint blue light that had brought her to the top of the steps. It was coming from a dip in the rock partially defended from the wind. It was little more than a hollow, and couldn't possibly have protected anyone against the avalanche, yet Sabira knew that if the frostsliver was glowing, there was hope.

'Uncle! Tserah!' Sabira called, and her spirits rose slightly when she heard an answering voice – a male voice. Uncle Mihnir!

Yet when Sabira dropped into the hollow, it struck her how quiet it was. There was no cheer or even a happy greeting. Both figures lay slumped on the floor, unmoving and propped up by the rock wall. The last of Sabira's joy rotted away.

'You made it,' the larger fur shape of her uncle said gruffly. He sounded so tired, like he had been carrying the mountain around these last hours. Sabira dropped down beside him.

'What . . . what happened? Is Tserah . . .'

Sabira couldn't finish the question. Tserah's pale, unmoving features made her dread the answer. She couldn't avoid it, though, for the glow around the frost-cleric's neck knew what she was really asking.

No, but her body is failing.

She scrambled over to the cleric, ignoring her leg's protests. Perhaps something her father had taught her could help Tserah before it was too late.

'What happened?' she asked again. A healer's first task was always to understand the injury.

'She did too much,' said Mihnir. 'Saved us, her and that frostsliver. It was like nothing I've ever seen.'

Mihnir's sad words were split by a small smile, as if he was already reminiscing about a friend long passed. Sabira's hands hovered over the fallen frost-cleric, frozen in hesitation. She knew almost nothing about a frostsliver's powers. It seemed to sense her confusion.

We held the avalanche.

Sabira's eyes widened. A frostsliver could do that much?

Power like that has a price, though. Tserah knew the consequences. She chose them. Our lives are bought by hers.

Sabira's breath caught, and she could feel fear swelling again. It was all she could do to get a few words of false denial out.

'She can't . . .'

Without me, she would not have survived this long. I

76

am all that's keeping her here now.

The musical voice was hardened to reality. Sabira wanted to believe that there was still a way for the woman to live, some talent she, Sabira, might have that could help the cleric, but what? The frostsliver guessed her thoughts.

Tserah will die, whatever you do. As will I – the loss of the bond kills. When a human dies, so does their frostsliver. Unless . . .

Sabira blinked. 'Unless what?'

Unless the bond is transferred.

Sabira's breathing quickened. What exactly was the frostsliver asking?

I need you to bond with me.

Shock seized Sabira. What could Tserah's frostsliver want with her, someone who couldn't even hold on to her own frostsliver? Wasn't the bond deeply personal? How could that be shared?

'Why me?' she asked. 'You must have thought I was dead, and Mihnir was right here.'

Mihnir wasn't chosen. You were.

Sabira had thought that she'd lost her chance to bond with a frostsliver for ever. Part of her felt a sudden sense of hope – but to do it like this, with Tserah's companion, and without the dying cleric's permission? It didn't feel right.

'What should I do?' she asked, turning to her uncle.

'It's not my decision to make,' Mihnir said guardedly.

'Would Tserah want me to do it?'

'Perhaps,' said her uncle. 'If you're successful, it will help keep you and the frostsliver safe. It's not right, but nothing about this is.' His reserve made Sabira question further.

'What aren't you telling me?'

It wasn't Mihnir who answered, but the frostsliver, cutting in with cold truth.

The loss of the bond kills. If I bond with you, she'll die.

Sabira's breath caught. It would kill Tserah? It seemed wrong – surely when there was still life, there was hope? Except that she had known too many nights when her father had returned from his surgery with the horror of failure about him, worrying over what he could have done differently and finding no answers. Sometimes there was no perfect path to take. Perhaps sensing her hesitancy, the frostsliver added,

We have little time.

'I . . . I don't think I can kill her!'

Think how I feel – I have been with Tserah for decades! I was nothing until I was with her – but I will not lose that. Besides, it will be me that has to do it, when I shift the bond. If this works at all.

It sounded angry and frightened, and Sabira realized that it really was a living thing too, not just an extension of Tserah, or some mindless servant. The frostsliver was dying, and afraid.

'I . . . I don't,' she stuttered.

You must decide now, before her body gives out.

Sabira shook in indecision. How could she do it? She'd never thought about taking another's life, even when threatened. What should she do? What would her parents do?

Her father would do it, for he was versed in making the hard surgeon's choice of saving one patient over another. Her mother would do it. She would have seen the necessity. But Sabira was not her parents, and the idea of killing Tserah, even to save the frostsliver, made her feel sick.

Finally, she made her choice, hating the logic. When it came down to it, Sabira could save one being and steal the last few minutes of life from another, or let both die.

'All right. All right, I agree. What do I do?' she asked.

Touch your bare skin to me, as you would have bonded your own frostsliver. I will do the rest.

Sabira worried at her glove until it came free, exposing her hand to the dreadful chill. Her fingers, though they felt like they might drop off in the cold, still managed to tremble a little from nerves.

She remembered Tserah's instructions on bonding: to clear her mind, remain calm and let the process work upon her rather than fight it. Fighting the mountain god was like standing against an avalanche, she'd told Sabira. You'd only be consumed.

The irony was that it had been Tserah who'd taught her, and now Sabira was going to kill her with that knowledge. She opened Tserah's neckline, hoping that at her touch the woman might stir, or give any sign of recovery, but there was nothing from the frost-cleric except shallow, sickly breathing.

Once the glowing cylinder was exposed, Sabira reached for it slowly, as if the thing might bite her. There was a strange cold shock as her flesh met ice, but Sabira pushed past it, curling her hand around the frostsliver and holding it tightly.

'What now?' she said, before she was cut off by an explosion in her head, a tidal force of power. A part of her tried to yank her hand away, break the connection, but she found that she could not move. Her entire body was locked in place.

She watched in terror as ice crystals started to form on her hand where it touched the frostsliver, creeping up her arm with terrifying speed. Her skin felt as if it was burning. She was sure that if she did not hold it back somehow, the sensation would consume her.

All Sabira knew was the strength of the glacier, flowing through the frostsliver and into her mind. Behind it something stirred, a beast of incredible depth, something old and powerful, knowing and vast, utterly alien – and yet, somehow, still a part of her, and she a part of it. A million or more separate, unified voices stormed through Sabira's mind. Aderast. The mountain god. More strange and wonderful than she had ever imagined.

She did the only thing that might possibly save her – she allowed the frostsliver's power to carry her, as if she was a part of that overwhelming flow herself, not something to be buffeted and smashed by it.

As her mind came back to her, she was able to sense that of another. Tserah, Sabira understood, was somewhere in here too. Thoughts flooded Sabira, and not her own. She felt Tserah's mind for a fraction of a moment, the woman's dreams and fears sliding into hers.

Regrets over not having the chance to start a family. Old loss – loved ones long gone. Loneliness, but a fierce optimism. Worries for the present, for the fate of nations, but faith in the future. In the frostslivers, in Aderast, in Sabira and her fellow chosen. In the knowledge and devotion the frost-clerics stood for. It came so fast, and all of it was slipping away.

In the rush it was hard to sense anything distinct, the life behind it dimming. However, in that sliver of consciousness Sabira connected with some echo of Tserah. Though it was disappearing into blackness, it still pushed through the barriers between them to speak in a feeling given form.

'Live well.'

Then the connection was severed, and Sabira fell into the abyss.

CHAPTER NINE

'Sabira!'

She awoke beside Tserah's still form with a start, unsure of how long she had been unconscious.

Then the truth hit her. Tserah was dead. Sabira didn't have to check to be sure, though she did anyway, listening for breath and pulse and finding none. Only the woman's body remained, the rest of her gone to Aderast. Gone to tell her story in the sleeping god's dreams.

'You're all right. She's gone, but it's all right, Sabira,' her uncle said. 'You had to do it.'

She pulled the cleric's hood down and cinched it

shut to cover Tserah's pale face, offering what respect she could. Besides, she couldn't bear to keep looking into her accusing eyes.

The only thing holding her together was those half-heard words – *live well*.

Her head was clearing and she began to feel the changes the bonding had brought. The most obvious was the glowing icicle hanging solidly in the slot of her leather-bound necklace, the frostsliver resting against her bare skin. She knew that never again would it lose contact, not until the day she died.

'It's so . . .' she began, but didn't have the words.

The frostsliver's ice felt oddly warm, like gentle steam against her skin. She didn't feel as cold as she had before either – it was as if a low fire within her resisted the chill.

None of it made Sabira's knee any better. Putting weight on it was like driving in needles, so instead she sat and drank in the new sensations. As she did, she registered an unfamiliar knot of thought behind her own. It was tightly coiled, but slowly its cool tendrils were uncurling.

Stop poking me. I'm settling in.

Sabira nearly jumped out of her skin at the voice chiming inside her. It felt like the frostsliver had slapped the back of her hand.

'You should eat,' her uncle murmured, interrupting. 'Get your strength up.'

She looked over at him, and noticed for the first time the pallor of his skin – a deathly pale, almost. She hurried to his side.

'Uncle, what's wrong?' she demanded, angry at herself for not attending him sooner.

'Took a tumble getting in here. Survive an avalanche, and get caught out by a little fall. Silly, really.'

He punctuated his words with a hacking cough, the kind that made you worry. She slid over to him and noticed his hands were positioned to cover a spot on his side. He resisted briefly when she tried to move them, but relented when she gave him her best glare.

Pulling Mihnir's furs loose was obviously painful for him, but she did not hesitate. A patient's discomfort was often the only way to find out what was wrong. When Sabira made an opening, she gasped. The flesh under his ribs was purpled with a mass of bruises and disturbingly swollen.

She'd seen that kind of injury before, and it was much worse than Sabira had guessed. He wasn't just bruised or exhausted, but seriously hurt. Whatever internal damage had been done was beyond her skills.

Her breathing quickened. Without the bonding path, rescuers from Adranna might be weeks away – if they were lucky. The food might stretch to that, but could Mihnir last as long? Sabira didn't think so. Not from the way her uncle lay slumped and barely moving after the strain of her examination.

Panic flickered in Sabira. Tserah had already paid for Sabira's life. She couldn't let Mihnir die up here too.

There may be no saving him. You must be prepared.

The voice, like the gentle tinkle of tapped icicles in her head made Sabira jump again. The frostsliver was hearing her thoughts! She tried to stand to fetch the pack and find out what she could use to help her uncle, but her knee twinged painfully again.

'I can't do anything with this,' she said, indicating her leg.

If only she had her father's equipment – and his expertise with medical bracing.

Then an idea came to her. She knew something of what frostslivers could do – this could work. Sabira would have explained, but found that the sentient ice was already moving, sliding across her skin in an undulating motion.

An interesting challenge.

The frostsliver's weird warm-coldness shivered down her torso and all the way to her knee, where it settled and solidified. Sabira could feel the weight being taken up by the frostsliver instead of the joint. It had formed the shape of the brace she had imagined.

Expecting another shooting pain, Sabira gently put a fraction of her weight on to her leg. There was discomfort, but not agony. Gingerly, she flexed her knee joint and smiled.

'That's amazing,' she admitted.

Yes. But it is not a miracle. You are still injured. You need time to heal.

'What about walking on it?' Sabira wondered. 'I don't want to make the injury permanent.'

This will keep the worst at bay.

It would have to do. Maybe it would be enough for her to do something. She looked at her uncle, who had shut his eyes. The pain was still obvious on his face, and she couldn't help thinking that Aderast seemed intent on claiming her and Mihnir. Just two more scarlet prayer flags in waiting.

Her uncle would go first, but Sabira would fare no better in the end. Without another plan, they would die out here above the Tears of Aderast. She didn't think the mountain would shed any more for her. Then, as she looked over to the skies above the mountain peak, where there had been blue between the clouds, Sabira saw the truth.

The blue had been filled in with swirling whiteness that licked and touched the mountainside, closing in even as she watched.

Sabira knew now that her growing feeling that the mountain hated her had to be right.

A blizzard was coming.

PART III

CHAPTER TEN

The blizzard looked almost peaceful from the valley top, a puff of white cloud in the distance. Soon, it would fall on them with all of nature's fury, and here they were defenceless against the storm.

We must go.

'But where to?' There was nowhere to go, no shelter in sight.

Down.

'What?'

The valley is our best chance. Hurry – do not let Tserah's sacrifice be in vain!

Sabira's heart slowed, ever so slightly. It was true. There could be some shelter down there. Maybe. If there weren't so many steps, and if Uncle Mihnir was in any state to walk them.

Move everything to the top of the stairs. Quickly.

Sabira wasn't sure why the frostsliver wanted that, but with no other choice, she dropped back into the hollow.

'Sabira?' Mihnir questioned. She cut him off before he could get any further.

'No time. Storm's coming. We have to go. Can you get up?'

The pack. You won't survive without it.

Heavy as it was, Sabira went to the thing and began hauling it. Her uncle, however, did not move, his face creased with pain.

Up, Packman Mihnir!

Even the frostsliver's words ringing out did nothing to rouse him. Sabira started forward.

The pack must go first. Come back for him.

'I won't leave him,' Sabira insisted angrily. After hurriedly moving the pack to the edge of the stairs down to the glacier, she charged back for her uncle.

As Sabira arrived, her eyes flicked to where Tserah's corpse cooled. A pang shot through her. She didn't like it, but she knew Tserah's body would have to be left behind. A desolate end, but it was the way of the Aderasti people. Her funeral would have seen it left out on the mountain anyway, returned to nature.

Sabira heaved Mihnir up with all her strength. She didn't quite know how she managed it, but after a minute's manhandling and pain, somehow they both flopped out of the hollow, just in time to be dusted with the first real lash of blizzard snow. They would be buried under more of the stuff, if she didn't hurry. When she had struggled and hauled her uncle up and over to the pack, the frostsliver instructed again.

Sit. You at the front.

'What?'

Now!

Sabira did so, positioning Mihnir behind so that he could wrap his arms around her. She felt his arms grasp her waist – he was partly conscious, at least. Looking down into the sickening depths of the glacier valley, she had a horrible feeling she could guess the rest of the plan.

You must do this.

Could she?

Yes. And you will.

The frostsliver liquefied, running down her leg. She felt it trickle over her foot. A moment later she felt the oozing sensation tear a hole in her layers of socks and wriggle through. The stitches in her boot creaked as they were forced apart by flowing ice.

To her shock, Sabira found herself raised on to a thin glassy pane, shaped for speed. Her boots were locked into place on it by clawing tendrils of ice, leaving her unable to escape as it spread and jammed under the front of the pack, turning it into a primitive kind of sled.

Her breath quickened as the frostsliver worked and extended, her heart beating even faster than the terrifying situation already deserved.

I need to take the strength from you.

There was no time to worry about exactly what that meant, as the frostsliver suddenly tipped forward, launching pack and its riders down the stairs. Sabira screamed, her voice snatched away by the whipping wind.

The gale pulled off her hood and raked through Sabira's hair with icy fingers, snow like needles against her bare skin. The frostsliver-sled descended faster and faster until Sabira was convinced they were falling straight down. The strange magic of the frostsliver hammered on her heart, and Sabira felt like she was running at full-pelt. The jaws of the valley opened up before her – the glacier's snow-covered bulk growing closer by the second. The frostsliver's voice sounded in her head, ringing in sudden fear.

I must not touch the glacier – I will be absorbed back into it. You will die!

'What?!' Sabira cried aloud. 'Why didn't you say that before?'

No time!

At this speed they'd never be able to stop before the end of the stairs – and the glacier was only seconds beyond that. Suddenly feeling very sick, Sabira remembered the sight of her own frostsliver sinking back into the ice, gone for ever.

'Retract, before we hit it!' she shouted.

Brace yourself.

Sabira wound in every muscle even tighter than she already had. The sled juddered, and the valley floor was rising fast. Moments before she hit the snow, she felt the frostsliver deform and shrink under her feet. The pack, Mihnir and Sabira tumbled through the air until Sabira's shoulder whacked into the snow. She slid a little, and opened her eyes to see the moving edge of the glacier just paces away.

Sabira couldn't move for shaking, unable to believe what they had done. She forced herself to her feet and went to Mihnir, who was lying on his back, blessedly still breathing. His eyes flickered as she knelt at his side.

'Are you all right?' she said.

'I've been better,' Mihnir grimaced.

I'm fine too – and you're welcome.

They didn't have long. The snowfall was getting heavier, and a cruel wind was starting to whistle, though they were more protected down here at the bottom of the valley. Sabira decided she'd have to leave the supply pack, and hope to recover it later. There was no way she could carry it as well as supporting her uncle.

'Up,' she demanded, though she knew it was a difficult thing she asked. Mihnir managed it, with her assistance, but he leant heavily on the steps when he was done.

Aderast howled a weather-tantrum at Sabira from the grey sky ahead. It didn't like where she was going. Neither did she. The landscape was starting to fade into the encroaching storm.

If the mountain really was a god, then it was a cruel one. Sabira debated cursing the place aloud, but decided not to risk further retribution.

Throwing her uncle's burly arm around her shoulders felt a little like picking up a log but, holding tight, Sabira struggled along the glacier shore, up the gentle slope of the valley towards the mountain peak, looking for cover.

The snow fought them, obscuring the way, getting into Sabira's hood and face within. She fought back as the minutes passed, but no shelter came into sight. Instead, the little colour remaining in the world drained away, replaced by the blankness of the blizzard. It turned out that death wasn't darkness, it was overpowering white.

On they went, until Sabira's arms felt like they might drop off at any moment. Mihnir stopped walking, and then stopped supporting his own weight.

Sabira wanted to demand that he move, that he keep going no matter what, but she knew he had already given everything he could. This was it. This was as far as they were going to get.

'You should have left me, found shelter on your own,' mumbled Mihnir, barely audible over the mountain's frenzy. Still dragging on his arm, trying to coax a little more out of him, Sabira shouted back,

'Just count yourself lucky I didn't! We're going to be fine, Uncle!'

She didn't believe it, though. In hours, or less, they would be dead.

Wait, that darker patch on the valley wall – was that . . . ? The frostsliver chimed happily, encouraging Sabira to take a closer look.

Hope kindling inside her, she found the strength to drag Mihnir closer. Salvation awaited in the form of a shadowed gash in the rock.

They stumbled into it, falling to the ground of the shallow cave as soon as they had passed the mouth. Sabira would very much have liked to sleep right there, but the mountain had other ideas.

Even several paces inside the cave, the storm continued to claw at them, like a predator trying to maul a mouse from its hole. The wind blasted in through the entrance, leaving the cave no more than a mild windbreak – at the back, however, a small curl in the passage offered some relief. She led her uncle further inside and settled him as far from the cave mouth as possible. He was exhausted and still deathly pale.

Sabira quickly found a place on the ground next to her uncle and huddled herself into a shivering ball. The lack of wind was one of the greatest presents she had ever received, and flakes of snow blew in from outside.

Sabira didn't like it, but she thought that she knew the answer. She remembered the last thing Tserah had done before her death – shielding that tiny hollow from the apocalyptic mass of the avalanche.

'Could we keep the storm out? The cold too, I mean?' Sabira said aloud, with more than a little trepidation.

Some of it.

'Should we try?' Sabira asked, feeling like the answer could go either way.

It won't be easy.

That was no endorsement, though when Sabira looked at Mihnir, she knew he wouldn't make it through the night if they didn't.

He may not anyway. Are you sure you want to risk us for that?

'We have to try.'

Getting a sense of the frostsliver's intentions through the bond, she held out her hand in anticipation. Once again her companion turned to flowing creature and back to solid object, pushing out from her

98

glove in a wide umbrella of ice that filled the crevice entrance with a thin, partly transparent barrier.

Sustaining the shield was not a pleasant sensation, the high heart rate an ugly beat of near pain in her chest – she felt as if she'd been running uphill for a week. She didn't want to think about the fact that such a feeling could grow strong enough to kill her, as it had Tserah. She had held back the incredible weight of the avalanche for only moments, and Sabira had no way to know how dangerous what she herself was doing was by comparison. Maybe the frostsliver could shield them all night, even through sleep, but Sabira was too wary to try it. It offered her an answer, unbidden.

It is inadvisable – but it probably won't kill you. Probably.

She peered out through her protection to the storm shrieking and blasting the mountainside, buffeting the frostsliver. Night was coming, and Sabira guessed that heavier snowfall was on the way. The blizzard didn't show any sign of abating, battering at their thin defence with ever greater strength. Storms like these had been known to last for days. If that happened, stranded here without their supply pack, they were done for.

They were in the grip of it now, with no end in sight. Sabira had seen how bad a blizzard could get even in the safety of Adranna.

This one had barely started, and it was only going to get worse.

CHAPTER ELEVEN

Night came, and it was harder than Sabira could have believed.

Cramped and cold, Sabira did everything she could to forget how bad a situation they were in. It was impossible with the heavy rhythm of her heart fuelling their only shield.

Mihnir had it worse, with his wound troubling him and no frostsliver bond to protect him from the chill. He shivered and shook, making noises of pain that a day ago Sabira would never have expected to hear from her tough, stoic uncle.

The only saving grace was that they were not out in

the snowstorm itself. Through the shield, the whirling whiteness was almost pretty, lit only by the frostsliver's soft glow. It was small comfort.

Frost-clerics supposedly kept the worst weather away, their prayers artfully written with calligraphy brushes and left in the elements for the mountain god. So much for that. Maybe Aderast hadn't thought much of their latest poetry.

There had to be some way to escape this nightmare. Some way to get home safely.

You may have to leave the packman behind. We'll never survive dragging him around the mountain.

Sabira saw the truth in it, but didn't like how coldly the frostsliver put it. The thing seemed to care for its own survival above all else.

'That's not an option. When the storm clears, we have to fetch the pack and divide it between me and Uncle Mihnir,' she said. 'After that, I'll climb across where the bonding path was. Then we can get help from Adranna and be back for Uncle Mihnir in a few days,' Sabira said, trying to convince herself as much as the frostsliver. A croaking from behind her showed that Mihnir had heard too – her part of the conversation, at least.

'That's a bad idea,' he said. 'The climb would kill you.'

Sabira knew he was almost certainly right. There just wasn't any other way to save him and she wasn't

101

going to give up. Her uncle must have seen the deter-
mination on her face, for he quickly wheezed,

'There might be another way.'

Sabira turned to face him. 'Another way? Isn't the
bonding path the only one between Adranna and the
glacier?'

'Tserah must have taught you that the glacier rises
from the depths of the mountain,' Mihnir said, though
the words did not come easily, 'but I expect you don't
know that people used to live up where it emerges,
near the mountain summit. There was a monastery
there once. Before the disaster of Aderast's Nightmare
put an end to it, centuries ago. No one could live there
through those conditions.'

He coughed a few times, before continuing,

'It's long abandoned now, but those of us who make
our lives climbing the mountain hear tales – have even
known a few adventurous sorts who claim to have seen
the old place. There will be shelter there, if you can
reach it, and maybe supplies. If you can build a big fire,
Adranna will see the beacon and send help.'

He wasn't offering options – he was trying to get
her to abandon him, just like the frostsliver was. Despite
the cold, she felt a flicker of heat rising in her. Sabira
fixed Mihnir with a stare and said as firmly as she could,
'You know you can't go anywhere. You think I'm going
to leave you to go and hide in a ruin until someone
comes in, what, weeks?'

If they came at all.

He didn't have the strength to argue, and for that Sabira was glad. In silence, she watched him slump lower and lower, between clear bouts of pain.

Eventually, he seemed to find peace enough to rest his eyes, and began a sleep just short of a coma. Sabira didn't know what to do for him, except hope that he could still wake in the morning. Until then, she had to keep him safe.

That left her alone with her mind's new resident, one she hadn't really spoken with properly yet. If she was going to be sharing her head with it, that had to change. The shield in front of her supplied an important starting point.

'If we're going to survive,' she asked, 'I need to know your limits.'

Tserah had pushed them too far, and Sabira feared doing the same. The memory of the woman pressed another pang of guilt through her as the frostsliver replied,

On top of your limits?

Those Sabira was already uncomfortably aware of.

As to shape, no. Only your imagination limits me. Our bond has other limits, though. I can only extend a certain distance. I am also not invulnerable. Fire is a danger, among other things.

'Is that . . . it doesn't sound like it will help that much.'

Had it been too much to hope for a secret power of flight, as she had once imagined as a child?

I have gone this far, abandoning my partner for life. I will not end because of your insecurities. Tserah would fight through this. So should you.

'Why did you leave her anyway?' Sabira found herself asking, the frostsliver's cold words building a fire in her. 'I've never heard of frostslivers jumping between people before.'

I . . . most don't.

'It wasn't to help us – you were afraid, weren't you?' she guessed. 'Afraid to die. You're supposed to be a piece of the mountain god – or at least one of Aderast's Tears. How can you be afraid?'

Were humans spun from Aderast's frost cocoons when the continent was young?

'Um . . . huh?'

Exactly. I don't know whether I'm a Tear of Aderast either. None of us know more about the world than you do. Even Tserah, the smartest woman I've known, did not know everything – and maybe you should remember that you don't either.

The frostsliver sounded pretty testy, so Sabira let the rest of her questions go for a while. It couldn't be pleasant for the frostsliver to remember the woman it had lost – the woman that Sabira was not.

In silence she kept up her vigil against the storm.

*

Hours passed, though Sabira didn't know how many. After a while, Sabira found that she could catch a good slice of the mountainside outside the cave if she sat just right, and shifted around in the small space until she could watch.

Then she looked up and thought that her tiredness was playing tricks on her.

Something had changed out there. What was that shape in the haze? She narrowed her eyes, peering closer. A rock? No, she didn't think that it had been there when they charged into the cave. Sabira was just starting to think that she must be mistaken – then it moved.

For a moment, Sabira didn't believe her eyes. There couldn't be anything living out in that. Could there? What if that shifting shadow was a person, a rescuer, or another traveller in trouble? A part of her wished it could be Tserah, brought back somehow from Aderast's embrace. She knew that it couldn't be, but the thought moved her anyway.

She had the frostsliver release the shield, the better to see whatever was out there, though she could feel a hum of dissent coming through the bond. As soon as it had moved to brace her knee, Sabira got up and peered around the edge of the crevice. There was something, she was sure of it. Not an animal – it was tall, like a person, though Sabira couldn't make out more than that.

'Hey!' she shouted over the noise of the blizzard, but if the shape heard her, it did not approach. In fact, it seemed to fade and Sabira feared that she was about to lose sight of it. No. No, she wasn't going to let that happen. If someone was alive out there, Sabira was not going to let them die because of her cowardice. Her hands tightened into fists as she summoned her courage.

Don't!

The frostsliver's voice was like a breaking pane of glass, but Sabira had already ignored the plea and darted into the tornado of white. She sprinted after the shadow.

Was that the shape of a person up ahead? It was impossible to be sure. To Sabira, the dark blot seemed too large to be human, but the storm distorted everything. It felt pointless to yell out, so great was the howl of the wind, though Sabira tried anyway.

'Hey! Stop!'

Sabira heard the frostsliver protesting in her head, but the meaning was lost to her, so intent was she on catching up to the shadow. Then she stumbled and almost lost her footing. By the time she recovered, all sign of the shadow had disappeared.

Sabira recognized the mistake she had made then, and fear began to chew at her. She didn't know the way back to the cave and Mihnir, and her tracks were obscured. Neither could she see any evidence that she had been chasing anything more than a mirage. Had her mind played a terrible trick on her?

Now she was lost, and if she continued in any direction, she could end up walking into a crevasse. She was lucky that it had not happened already. Sabira turned, peering through the storm, searching for anything familiar.

She stopped suddenly. There was something up ahead, something too big and solid to be a mirage. A horrible sinking feeling filled her stomach.

The shadow let out a sound that no human could produce, something between a roar and a cracking, grinding wail. Sabira turned and ran blindly in the opposite direction, content to never find out what kind of creature had made it. As she pelted away in terror, her mother's stories of yeti prowling the mountain flashed through her mind.

As she took a moment to look back for the monster that might be pursuing, Sabira's foot hit something moving. She saw a blur of white before sprawling forward on to all fours. Panicking, she scrabbled around for purchase. Then sense came back to her, and Sabira realized what had happened.

It wasn't something moving at all, but the rock of the mountain. She must've wandered on to the glacier, and now she had had fallen off and back on to its bank. She tried to catch her bearings, but everywhere was a curtain of white. For all she knew, she was on the wrong side of the glacier.

If that monster was after her and could find her in this, there was nothing she could do about it. She couldn't flee to the cave – even if she was walking in the right direction, she might pass right by the place without seeing it.

Sabira crouched low and blundered onwards, searching for any kind of shelter. She found a freezing rock about half her height, and hunkered down beside it. There couldn't be more than a few hours left before the dawn. Maybe then she could find her way back more easily. Maybe.

I *told you not to leave the cave*, the frostsliver said icily.

The night passed slowly and in terror. In every snow flurry Sabira saw shades of things that weren't there, clutching her furs tightly around her as she shivered, even when the frostsliver covered her torso in a thin, warm shield.

Once, she saw a light from above, and thought for a moment that the storm was breaking, that she was finally seeing the sky twinkling down at her, but she was not so lucky.

It wasn't the stars brightening the night, or the dawn. It was a yellow fire on the mountain high above. That was what it looked like anyway – though from what Mihnir had told her, there shouldn't have been anyone else alive up there. Whatever the source, it was too far away to reach. Then the blizzard's white clouds crowded in again, and the light disappeared.

She forced herself to stay awake while the slow, cold torture worked its hooks into her, for Sabira knew that sleep had to be fought off at all costs. It was the road to death, paved with the comfort of oblivion.

On into the night she sat, staring into the abyss.

CHAPTER TWELVE

Dawn came, and with it the light, but the blizzard was not done – although it was weaker than it had been in the night.

Sabira's bones felt locked in place and the exposed skin of her face was seared by the wind. She fought against her body's protestations and stood.

At least she had not been eaten by yeti.

Not yet, the frostsliver helpfully interjected.

In fact, she hadn't seen another hint of that huge yeti-like shadow. She hoped it hadn't eaten its fill of packman while she was gone. That horrible thought was enough to get her moving, and Sabira pushed away from her rock.

She looked up at Aderast. The light she had seen last night seemed almost unreal, like part of a dream – but it had been there, hadn't it?

If it was a dream, I dreamt it too.

Sabira let the question go for now, and moved off, staying low and moving slowly, keeping one hand trailing along the valley wall so that she couldn't get lost.

It was lucky she did, for she found that her first instinct was leading her in the wrong direction – back to the steps rather than to Mihnir. When she saw her error, Sabira chose to make use of it, and went all the way there to fetch the supply pack.

The bulky pack had almost been buried by snow, and only barely jutted out. Sabira had to dig it up. When she was finished, collapse seemed very appealing. She couldn't, though, not here in the still-falling snow, so she began the arduous process of moving the supplies up to the cave.

Choosing to drag the heavy thing instead of attempting to carry it, Sabira spent a good half an hour pulling the cursed bag up the mountainside, all the while worrying about what she would find when she got there. By the time she had almost reached the cave, her exhaustion had caught up with her, and she was sweating beads of saltwater that did their best to freeze on her skin.

Upon entering, Sabira's eyes darted about for any

111

evidence of a struggle, but found none. She crept slowly to the back, and saw to her relief that the crevice remained full of the fur-shrouded packman she had left there.

Mihnir had not been eaten by a yeti – but had he survived the night? Sabira feared the worst when she didn't see any movement from her uncle. Then the mound of furs made a small noise.

'Sabira . . .'

Thank the mountain. She smiled at him, her frozen features cracking painfully.

'It's all right,' Sabira said. 'I'm here now, and I bring gifts.'

The sight of her hauling the pack into view was enough to get Mihnir to smile weakly too, though Sabira wasn't going to take his health for granted. After moving around so much last night with internal injuries, her uncle was lucky to be alive.

There was a lot to do, and she began by extracting the healer's kit from the pack, before retrieving the rest of its vital bounty. There were several thick blankets inside. Sabira wrapped Mihnir in most of them, before securing another in place over the crevice opening, blocking the worst of the wind.

As she worked, she told Mihnir of everything he'd missed, including the strange light she'd seen on the mountain. When Sabira was done, her uncle allowed himself to slump down even further, looking relieved.

'I was so worried about you,' he said, 'but you're safe now.'

'Not really,' said Sabira, thinking of where they both still sat.

'No, I suppose not. I wish I could help you. Protect you. I ... I'm sorry.' He paused, then added, 'I can't go any further.'

Sabira couldn't say anything to that, instead going to the healer's kit and rooting around inside, tears blurring her eyes. The frostsliver was quiet in her mind, but she was surprised to sense a gentle sympathy through the bond.

The whistling of the wind was dying away. The blizzard had finally blown itself out. It was good news. It should be good news. Sabira's fingers fell still, unable to find an excuse to continue. There was truth to face. She knew what her uncle was going to say before he said it.

'You're going to have to leave me – not to get help. I'm done for, but you aren't.'

'Don't talk like that,' she pleaded. He ignored her and continued,

'You said you saw fire above. The only place up there is the old monastery. I don't know why anyone would be there, but that's your way out of this. It's the only way. All you have to do is follow the glacier to sanctuary.'

It was a better hope than trying the bonding path.

That route would kill her, she felt sure. That wasn't enough, though. Her chances were poor wherever she was. Mihnir's were zero if she did what he said.

'I don't want to leave you,' she said, but something he'd said sparked in her mind. *Follow the glacier to sanctuary.*

'You know, in the story,' she began slowly, 'the First Bonded descended through the mountain and found their way to the glacier's source. They made it out from the passages beneath and founded Adranna. If they could follow it back through the mountain, so could someone else.'

'Sabira, that's . . . a story. A legend. Who knows how much of it is true?'

'Some. It has to be – how could it not be when the frostslivers exist? You're a Tear of Aderast – tell him!' she said, directing the last question at the frostsliver hanging around her neck.

He's right. Going inside the mountain would be very dangerous. Deadly, even.

It wasn't what Sabira had wanted to hear, but she pressed on.

'Somebody did those things. The First Bonded found the source of the glacier alone. Then there's the Deep Explorers. They broke Aderast's Nightmare and saved everyone from its wrath. They all found their way down through the mountain and out, every one of them! It could be the only way to get to Adranna in time to send someone to rescue you. It could be your only chance.'

'I . . . Sabira. Swear that you won't do this. The monastery, you've got a chance there, but inside the mountain . . . no one will find you.'

His words chipped at her wall of resolve, but did not break through.

'I swear I'll be safe,' she told him, although she knew she couldn't keep the promise. Was she really considering this? What was wrong with her?

I wonder that too.

No – it had to be done. If the mountain wanted any more of her family, it was going to have to fight her for them.

Mihnir obviously wanted to argue, but didn't seem to have the strength. Discussing it further wasn't appealing, so instead of dwelling on the plan, Sabira acted on it, breaking down the supply pack with renewed vigour. Even with her hands hard at work, she kept thinking: how was she going to do this alone?

Not alone – but you had better not get me killed.

That was small comfort. Sabira packed in silence, dividing the supplies while Mihnir looked blearily on. Fortunately they had food enough for a few days, and more than enough snow to melt and drink if necessary. She made sure to move the most easily digestible food to his pile, and the most energy rich food to hers. They were both going to need it. After a while, her uncle seemed to realize what she was doing and why. He shook his head and said,

'You should take it all.'

She did not stop her sorting.

'Sabira!'

She stopped, looked up, and speared him with determined eyes.

'I'm not leaving you with nothing. I won't. Our family has lost enough out here,' she said, knowing that nothing he could say would change her mind. Mihnir opened his mouth, but Sabira cut him off.

'There's no point objecting,' she said, trying to keep tears back. 'It's not like you're in any shape to stop me.'

Her voice shook as she spoke, though she ended firmly.

Mihnir's mouth opened and shut a few more times as he searched for an answer. Finally, he nodded in agreement. He even smiled slightly through his pain, in what Sabira thought might be pride.

After separating out supplies for Mihnir, she stuffed a bag with as much as she could reasonably carry, knowing that every extra provision, length of rope or fire starter might mean the difference between life and death.

'If the pain gets bad,' she said, showing him the healer's kit, 'open this and take a little of the fern-like plant with the tiny blue flowers – but no more than a bite every few hours. It should help.'

He smiled weakly, and then began to cough. Watching him, Sabira feared the worst, but the fit subsided after a few moments.

'I will take a small dose now, if you don't mind,' Mihnir added, when he was able. She fed him a small portion of the herb for him to chew, and after a minute he relaxed a little, the pain lifting temporarily.

'Just hang on. Try not to move much – but eat and drink, keep your strength up. I'll be back with help soon,' Sabira offered quietly. He nodded, though she wasn't sure if he was really hearing her, or if the herb was beginning to affect him, for next he said,

'They really did make the right choice with you . . .'

Her uncle's last words were quieter, for he was already drifting towards uneasy sleep. Sabira wasn't sure the man knew what he was saying, though it was a comfort all the same.

Getting up, she scooted to the hanging blanket and peeked out. Only a few flakes of snow greeted her, and the barest gust of wind. The storm truly had given in.

We should go.

She turned to Mihnir, his strong body laid low, probably never to rise again. Sabira had hoped to find the right words for their parting, to say something to give her uncle hope that this was not the end, but nothing came.

'Goodbye,' she said softly.

Mihnir stirred, and Sabira's breath caught – she

hadn't thought he would hear her.

'Be safe – and watch for snow-spines,' he croaked, already half-asleep. *That same silly joke again*, she thought as he closed his eyes. Sabira didn't say anything. She couldn't, for fear of the emotion that might spill out. Instead, she just hefted her burdens on to her back, and brushed her way past the hanging material to the world outside.

Sabira didn't look back. She didn't want to see the man she was abandoning. Her kind, funny uncle whom she was never going to see alive again.

CHAPTER THIRTEEN

You should not feel so guilty.

Sabira almost tripped over her own boots at the mental voice. She had only been going a few minutes, all of them lost in doubt. It certainly didn't feel right.

'I just abandoned him,' Sabira retorted. 'He's probably going to die in there.' Her voice choked at the thought.

Better than us dying too. And he wanted us to go, even though he doesn't agree with your 'plan' about going through the mountain.

'You're not just telling me what I want to hear?'

She hated when adults did that.

Do you like what I'm saying that much? No?

It paused to let that sink in.

I would not lie to you. We could not stay with him and survive.

On. On. On she travelled across the white incline, steps accompanied by the cracking glacier beside her. There was some kind of voice in that, Sabira felt sure, though the actual words fled from her.

'I wonder,' said Sabira as a thought occurred to her, 'if my frostsliver – the one I lost, I mean – is in there still.'

It is possible. The frostsliver you cut could be meltwater by now, or back in the heart of the mountain.

Sabira was glad of one thing: her knee felt a lot better. The frostsliver had told her the truth – that brace was a blessing.

She needed it too, as her hike stretched on, the gently sloping valley giving way to steeper ground where the glacier plunged down small ridges and cliffs. To begin with, ascending them wasn't so bad. It was even a nice change of pace to have to clamber up instead of continually trudging.

Then the small cliffs got larger, until they were taller than Sabira's head. It got to the point where a fall from one could easily have killed her. She continued nevertheless – what else could she do? She had faced death already after all.

Sabira's mind kept returning to painful questions. How was Mihnir doing? Was he still alive? Should she enter the mountain, with so little hope? Did she have the supplies to last the trip? How was she going to find the way through Aderast? Was it even possible to save Mihnir?

Enough! Tserah never used to bombard me with worries like this.

'I . . . I'm sorry I'm not her.' Sabira pulled herself up a steep ledge to another snowy platform.

No reply, but she sensed a flash of mingled pain and guilt through the bond.

Sabira trudged on. 'I know you didn't want this, but you did ask me to save you.'

A fact one might come to regret.

Suddenly, the snow in front of her erupted in a thin plume, and from within something narrow and whip-fast shot at her head so quickly that Sabira had no time to dodge. The frostsliver was quicker, flashing up her body and out to her hand, where it took the shape of a falcon, its hooked beak biting down on her attacker and deflecting it.

Without the brace, pain lanced through Sabira and her leg buckled, sending her to one knee and wrenching the frostsliver to one side. The thing in its grasp ripped free, and the white, leathery tendril whipped around for another attack, striking at Sabira with more speed than seemed possible. She sprawled forward under the slash but immediately it began winding its single deadly limb back into its lair for another attempt.

One nick of that stinger, that was all it would take. She'd be paralysed and defenceless as the snow-spine sucked her dry. She wanted to flee – but she'd be running in the wrong direction, the way up still blocked by the snow-spine.

Instead, Sabira pushed herself up and on before the creature could attack again, fighting through the pain. Scrambling past the hole that held the snow-spine's tuberous mass, Sabira sprinted for the tall ledge up ahead. The steep terrain made the distance too far to cover, and over her beating heart, Sabira heard the swishing sound of another strike behind her.

She spun, knowing that she had to fight. Sabira just hoped that the frostsliver was fast enough. She started her slashing motion with an empty hand, aiming for the air below the stabbing stinger.

The blade of an icy hunting dagger formed in her hand the moment the snow-spine was about to connect, its edge glowing and keen. It severed the stinger cleanly in a spray of pinkish liquid, and Sabira dodged frantically out of the way as the tendril-tip fell, separated from its owner.

Then her foot slipped, and she was tumbling back down, bouncing and scraping everything as she blurred past the snow-spine and on. Something painfully sharp got to her face through her hood, but Sabira was too disorientated to care.

Finally, she slid to a halt on the snow, but was given only a second of safety before the stinger came bouncing after her, forcing her to roll aside with a squeak of fear.

The thing squished down, flopped and writhed impotently beside her for a moment, and then lay still. For long moments Sabira couldn't move, lying back and breathing out her relief.

As she began to recover from the rush of her near-death experience, Mihnir's joking warnings came back to her, and Sabira had to laugh. When was the last time someone had reported a snow-spine? Years? They'd been dying off ever since Aderast's Nightmare birthed them into the world – though apparently not quickly enough. Mihnir had probably thought she would never even see one. The blood pumping in her ears quieted enough for her to hear the frostsliver exclaim,

Mountain's blood and spit, that was close!

'Didn't know you used such language,' Sabira said, stifling a giggle. She heard a ding in her head that could have been an embarrassed cough.

We are lucky. Nothing is broken.

Sabira felt bruised enough to think the frostsliver must be wrong. The words prompted her to pick herself up, though, before peering back up at where she had fallen from. Only when she saw the snow-spine's pus-oozing tendril lying motionless next to its hole did she begin to calm. Dead. It had to be. One encounter was enough for a lifetime.

Her breathing slowed and her mind drifted back to their conversation before the snow-spine. 'Do you really regret bonding with me?' she asked quietly.

No – I should not have spoken like that.

Time to move on – but there was something she should do first. Gingerly, Sabira picked up the amputated stinger and examined it. The disgusting thing had come away cleanly, and its deadly poison sac was still attached, a bulbous pale growth below the point of the sting.

The venom would be a prize for any healer, and Sabira paused to wrap the organ in cloth and stow it in the medicine bag. Her father would be doubly pleased to see her if she returned with that. Everyone would be surprised to find that any were left – and pleased to see one less deadly snow-spine on the mountain. They were the last trace of Aderast's bad dream – the catastrophic weather it had made disappeared long before Sabira's parents were born.

You are cut.

Sabira panicked for a moment that the snow-spine had got her after all, before she realized to her relief that it must have been the impact during the tumble.

When she touched her cheek, Sabira's glove came away bloody, and caused a spark of pain in her cold-numbed flesh. It felt like more than a scratch, and her concern was proved right when the frostsliver's voice echoed in her woozy head,

It needs stitches.

Wonderful, Sabira thought, though she didn't protest. She had seen too many wounds not taken care of properly. With no one else to do the job, she retrieved needle and thread from her pack, and a tiny bottle of disinfecting alcohol. She was going to have to sew herself up.

With a wince, she dabbed her cut with the alcohol, before preparing her needle with the same stuff. Her gloves were too clumsy for the work, so she pulled them off, exposing her fingers to the cold. Carefully, she touched the still-bleeding cut, gauging its position and depth. She moved the needle in, tensing in expectation of pain.

A little further up.

Sabira almost stabbed herself. Instead she sighed, moved her hand as indicated and through gritted teeth said,

'Thank you.'

Before the frostsliver could interrupt her again, she got to work. Pinning the curved needle through her skin hurt less than she had expected, but more than enough to make her hand shake. She took a moment to steady, and then pulled the thread through after the needle until the tiny knot at the end lodged.

Careful now. You only have so much blood to lose – and it's as much mine as yours.

She did not respond, just gently continued pulling the flesh of her cheek together, feeling her eyes water and trying not to twitch at the pain. She tightened the stitch completely, before taking a heartbeat or two to breathe and wait for the pain to lessen.

Just two or three more to go.

Eventually, she finished, packed away her tools and allowed herself a brief rest. As Sabira calmed, she realized that her fingers still had blood on them, as did her gloves. She did her best to clean them in the snow, staining it red.

'Here, another offering for you – as if you haven't had enough already,' she said, returning part of herself to Aderast. Some said that such things placated the mountain, and Sabira would take any mercy she could get. She looked up to where the monastery had to be.

'We're going to get there. We're going to make it,' Sabira said.

Not if we have more encounters like that.

She sighed, sick of the blunt voice in her head – though it did have a point.

'Is there a way we can talk more face to . . . whatever?' she asked, desperate for a more normal conversation. 'This is still all a bit weird to me.'

Before she had finished, the frostsliver's shiver formed into a miniature ash-cat on her palm, rendered in ice that poked through her glove's seams and much like the toy she had once owned.

'Did you get that from me?' she asked, not sure if she was comfortable with her past being an open book for the frostsliver to read.

Mostly.

The thing's tiny ice-mouth clinked the word out. Sabira stared at it, emotions pushing in different directions. It wasn't trying to upset her, she decided. Just to make her feel comfortable. She bit back some of the more hostile things she had been thinking of saying.

'Look,' she began, 'this isn't working.'

You and I may be struggling to work together, but . . .

'The brace! The knee brace isn't working. It's keeping me from getting permanently injured, but if you need to be something else in a hurry, it's going to get us killed! I need to be able to walk normally!'

There are risks involved, but I could simply numb you.

Instantly the pain in her knee vanished, a bone-deep chill replacing it. Sabira flexed the joint. It didn't bend quite as easily as it should, but it didn't hurt.

'This could work.'

I am not sure that this is wise. Remember, I am supressing the pain and stiffening the joint, but you are not healed. This will not prevent further damage.

She thought of Kyran, and everything that had

happened to him. How could she not? The memory hardened her resolve, and she nodded in acceptance.

Better injured than dead.

A few hours later, Sabira reached the base of a cliff many times larger than those she had scaled so far. She looked up at its dizzying height and gulped.

It was a sheer wall of rock, pitted, rough and not far off vertical. This was not an obstacle to be overcome in minutes, but a challenge even for a seasoned climber, and it would take an hour or more to ascend.

There was something else to be seen atop the cliff, barely visible but clear enough to send Sabira's emotions spinning. It was the wall of a building, weathered and old, but unmistakeably created by human hands.

'Part of the monastery?' Sabira wondered aloud. It had to be. A single crystalline *ding* rang in the back of her mind, like a fine glass bell being lightly struck. Apparently, the frostsliver agreed.

A kindling of hope caught within Sabira. There had been someone up there last night, she was certain: it was just possible that rescue might be near.

Still, this was going to need more than just careful climbing. The frostsliver sent an answer skittering into Sabira's mind.

Smiling, she held out an open hand and felt the frostsliver slither towards it, forming a spike of ice similar to a climbing piton.

The shining spike stabbed easily into the rock, nothing like any normal knife. Sabira set her weight on it and heaved upwards. She wouldn't have called it easy or safe, but it worked.

All she had to do was find a single handhold for her other hand, lodge her feet as best she could, pull and stab. She did it again, taking herself fully off the ground.

Only a thousand repeats to go.

Over and over she plunged the ice spike into the rock and heaved her body upwards. Soon it became so monotonous and so tiring that she felt a fall would almost be worth the relief.

Daylight was on the verge of dying. Sabira tried very hard not to look down, but when she did she felt her stomach quake. Her muscles were on fire, and a drop would be deadly. How much longer could she hold on? That was the thing about climbing: the most dangerous part was always when you were nearly done. Sabira pushed on through the last stabs of frostsliver into rock, and just as her arms were starting to fail, her hand met the cliff edge.

Relief flooded her and she hauled her lead-heavy limbs over the lip of the cliff. Sabira felt the frostsliver liquefy back into her clothing, settling on her necklace as if it too were resting.

Sabira looked up, and found nothing she wanted to see. All this way, through falls and cuts and nearly

129

becoming prey, and here was her reward.

Everywhere she looked there was ruin, stark and frosted, or part buried in snow. If there ever had been fire up here, it was gone, snuffed out by the cold, the mountain and time.

PART IV

CHAPTER FOURTEEN

Sabira stood on the ledge for a long time, staring at the ruins. The slow in and out of her chest was her only motion as she took in the silent, desolate landscape. No one was here.

She had half a mind to turn and leap from the cliff, but eventually she settled her breathing and stepped away from the edge.

She started walking around the huge site, which was strewn with rubble and the tumbledown walls of the many small buildings that had formed much of the monastery. It was hard to imagine this had ever been a bustling place of worship. She waited for the frostsliver to say something to convince her that this was just a setback. It remained silent. Sabira didn't want to hear it anyway. Her horror had burnt away into a kind of hollow ache.

Heading through the silent, snow-covered ruins, Sabira tried to stay practical.

'What happened to this place?' she asked the frost-sliver. 'Do you know?'

Time?

It sounded almost sad.

Sabira was inclined to agree. The buildings' destruction seemed to have been wrought by neglect. Ornate conical roofs had collapsed sideways, wooden pillars had decayed and brought down everything they supported.

'Mihnir did say that Aderast's Nightmare forced this place to be abandoned,' said Sabira.

It seems that no one has taken care of it since.

Though the plateau had been spared the avalanche, snowdrifts clutched at the remains of the monastery's outbuildings. Where they emerged from the snow, the ruins looked less like human constructions and more like the bones of some long-dead giant beast.

But as Sabira tramped through one large building, its high-domed roof long gone, she found something else between the ancient rubble: the remains of camp-fires, and footprints. She crouched, peering at the marks. They looked human, but how could so many people have been up here? The footprints were fresh too – preserved in the patchy snow and earth by the day's calm, clear weather. Beside the remains of the campfire were animal bones picked clean after cooking. Whoever it was must've been here recently. But why? Sabira stood up and kept looking, keeping a keen eye out for more details as she walked in and out of the shells of what once was.

Soon she came to where the glacier spilt from the mountain wall. It looked as if the main part of the monastery had been built around the glacier into the very rock of Aderast, but it was blasted to rubble now. Could there still be a way into the caverns through that? It was too dark to see.

Nearby, she found an open area that left her even more confused. At its centre lay a huge blackened pile. Someone had indeed set a pyre, a big one, and let it burn down. Sabira prodded at the ashes, finding a few unscathed objects among the mess: pieces of furniture, and a large number of books, though they were too badly damaged to read.

What a waste.

Sabira had to agree. She searched everywhere in the half-light, but found nothing beyond the remains of the large campsite. Whoever had been here last night, they had left all their litter behind to mark their passing. That wasn't like Aderasti, who believed the sacred mountain should be kept pristine, save for the bodies of the dead. Something about that niggled at her. Things didn't add up. Vanishing people on the mountain, in a dead monastery. An avalanche where there should never have been one. She was starting to wonder if her troubles might not solely be the work of the mountain after all. It almost made sense, but she was so tired. She felt like it should be obvious, but things just wouldn't slot together in her head.

The last of the daylight was fading, and Sabira was exhausted.

Better camp here for the night. Save your strength for the morning.

As she headed towards the less ruined outhouses, Sabira began gathering what she could scavenge. It wasn't much, but she couldn't afford to be choosy. The meat scraps clinging to bones seemed unspoilt, though Sabira still wasn't sure what any of it was. Risking eating it didn't seem like the best idea, but she stored the stuff nevertheless. The day might come when it was all she had.

She even found a half-empty little metal flask, full of some dark liquid that smelt like something her parents would never have let her drink. After one swig, she could see why – the strong spirit tasted awful. She kept the flask anyway.

Urrgh.

Sabira ignored the frostsliver's disapproval. When she had explored as far as she could make herself,

Sabira picked an old storage building with four walls and part of a roof for her camp. As she entered, she knocked something skittering across the stone floor with her foot.

She bent to pick up the object, heart in her mouth. Though it was missing limbs and half destroyed by exposure, Sabira still recognized it as a child's toy ash-cat. She would have known it anywhere. Kyran had held it last.

Her eyes stung with tears as she held the evidence of her brother's passing. Why had he been here? Most assumed that, because of his leg, he had fallen from the bonding path into one of its many chasms, his body never to be found, but Sabira had always guessed that Kyran had made it to the Tears of Aderast, and been rejected by the glacier. He never got the training on how to bond that she'd had, after all. Opinions varied as to what that did to a person, but none of them sounded pleasant and death was a common guess. Now it seemed likely that she had been right.

Why – and how – had he come all the way to the monastery? Where had he gone from here? What had happened to him? Nothing good, that was for sure – he had never come home after all.

Best to let it go.

Maybe. But while it was painful knowing that Kyran had come so far, only to fail, it also gave her an odd sense of clarity. She would not follow in his footsteps, she vowed, slipping the broken toy into a pocket, holding it close as if it was a talisman. She slumped down, head in her hands, fighting the urge to cry. She didn't want to be that person. She wanted to be like the heroes in tales, able to push on no matter what. Grief threatened to drown her, though, and even the constant presence of the frostsliver did nothing to help her forget how alone she was.

Sleep did not come easily, and when it did it was full of bad dreams.

Sabira woke in the night, certain she was being watched from beyond her small campfire. The shapes of the ruins looked strange in the darkness, and there was something moving in the shadows. She stood quietly. If danger was out there, she refused to sit and wait for it to fall upon her.

Careful.

Creeping through the darkness with only the dancing fire at her back, she strained her eyes at the undulating motion that had caught her attention. Only steps away, it occurred to her that there might be more than one snow-spine on the mountain – and if this was one of them, she was dead. For a long, skipped heartbeat Sabira couldn't help but see the twisting shape as a striking tendril, and her hand clenched, ready to swing the frostsliver, already transformed into a hunting knife.

Then, as her eyes adjusted, she saw the ancient, raggedy remains of a prayer flag, flapping in the wind. Sabira shivered, and went back to her fire. There was nothing here, she told herself, nothing except bones and ice. She should try and get some much-needed sleep.

She did her best, but she kept waking, the fire closer to being burnt out each time, eventually no more than embers in the dark. Each time she turned over and drifted back into blackness. Then, through the haze of a dream, a glass-sharp word cut into her rest.

Sabira.

For a moment, her bleary brain didn't understand what was going on, or where she was. Shouldn't she be in bed, with its fur covers and its view over the city? The frostsliver's voice sounded again, this time more urgently.

Sabira! Wake up.

'What? Why?' she asked, still only half awake. Sabira cracked open her eyelids to darkness and frost, but no understanding. The frostsliver grew more urgent.

Hide, Sabira! Something is coming.

No, that couldn't be right. She was still on the mountain, in the deserted ruins. She had to be dreaming. The frostsliver began to ding loudly in her head.

This is no nightmare. For both our sakes, move!

She bounded up, unbalanced but awake, seeking

about for the source of danger and seeing none.

It's coming!

Hastily, Sabira kicked snow over her fire's embers, extinguishing the last of its light. She held still for a moment, watching nervously – more so since she could feel the frostsliver's own anxiety through the bond.

There *was* something moving out there. Not a prayer flag either. This shadow was too large, too slow. Sabira's heart jumped into her mouth as she realized that it was coming closer.

She backed away and slipped out of an opening on the opposite side of the building, doing her best to blend in with the shadows. She couldn't run, not in this darkness, on icy ground – not if she wanted to avoid breaking her neck.

It is getting closer!

The frostsliver sounded almost panicked. Sabira crept faster across the snow, wincing at the crunch of her footsteps, looking for something to conceal her. A handful of paces away was a flat-roofed structure that might once have been a large shed. It was partly open to the elements now, but the roof seemed intact and, crucially, it was tall enough that she couldn't see on to it. She made her way over as quickly as she dared, grabbed the first promising handhold and started up.

She scaled the small building quickly, driven by fear. Soon, she lay stomach-down on the building's cold, flat roof. Without looking up, no one would have a hope of finding her, and if they did, she might still be able to scoot away from the edge before being spotted. Doing that now would probably be wiser, but she had to see what was out there.

A minute passed with nothing except the wind for company, and Sabira was starting to hope that she and the frostsliver had been mistaken when she saw something stump into the space beneath her in the gloom. The moment she caught sight of it, Sabira pressed herself even harder into the rooftop, trying to make herself part of it, her heart racing in terror.

That was no human. The form was all wrong, bulkier and harder somehow. There was none of the fuzzy outline that cold weather furs provided, and it didn't move like someone chilled by the mountain. It stood easily, looking at home in the bitterly cold weather and, Sabira saw, there was a faint shimmer to it, giving the thing an unearthly look.

Starlight was not enough to fully make it out, and for that Sabira was glad. If she could see it properly, it might see her. She didn't breathe as she watched, and feared her heart was beating loud enough that anyone could hear it, let alone this thing. Its head turned this way and that, and Sabira had the horrible feeling it had sensed something. She silently prayed that it was not her.

Her eyes tracked the shape as it moved, not daring

to shift her head in case the motion was enough to attract its attention. Only when it turned – agonizingly slowly – and strode away did Sabira's muscles relax. She rolled back on to the roof and allowed herself a quiet gasp of air. Minutes passed in silence. She listened. Listened. Nothing.

What had it been?

A *yeti*?

Sabira shook her head in disbelief. Some said the yeti were the mountain's guardians, disposing of those Aderast deemed unworthy. Some said they were remnants of Aderast's Nightmare, like the snow-spines. Some said both – but all agreed that the yeti were dangerous monsters. Monsters that ate human flesh. She gulped. Well, it was gone now, and good riddance. Sabira was happy for it to remain a mystery, so long as she didn't ever have to see the thing again. It would be just another tale of mysterious yeti on the mountain, if she could make it back to civilization. If Aderast's defenders wanted her to leave, she was happy to oblige.

'How did you know it was there?' she asked the frostsliver. It didn't have eyes of its own after all.

I sensed its approach. It felt . . . wrong.

Sabira didn't know what that meant, but she was glad that the frostsliver had been able to warn her. She prepared to ask the obvious question, but the frostsliver got there first.

I don't sense it any more. As far as I know, we are safe.

Sabira didn't believe that for a second. Aderast seemed to want her dead, and if the mountain wanted her blood, what could stop it? There was nothing in the world that was going to get her to move off this roof for the rest of the night. Not with the yeti still out there somewhere, stalking unseen.

CHAPTER FIFTEEN

The morning broke with a nasty crack.

For a frightening moment, Sabira thought that the monster had returned to devour her, and begun by breaking her bones. Then she saw the fallen piece of ice nearby, broken off under the slight heat of the morning light. She relaxed slightly and climbed carefully down from her hiding place. As she went to collect her things back at the camp, the frost-sliver demanded,

Are you still determined to go inside the mountain?

'How else are we going to get home?' Sabira retorted. 'Mihnir needs us to do this.'

The frostsliver made a noise like breath over a glass – a huff of displeasure, Sabira thought. She ignored it and moved on, mentally cataloguing her remaining supplies as she headed towards the mountain face. She knew she had enough food for a few days at least, but there were other worries too.

How long could her water reserves last down in the darkness? There was always the glacier, she thought wryly, as she walked beside it. However, not only would that be wrong, but it also seemed pretty unwise. Who knew what that not-ice would do to her insides?

I could show you.

'Show me?' she asked dubiously. The frostsliver shifted its position slightly, indicating a move towards Sabira's face – and her mouth.

'What would happen?'

To me? Nothing much. I am immune to a little stomach acid.

Sabira let the obvious question spin around her head for the frostsliver to hear.

You would be all right. For a while. I think.

She was starting to think that comments like that were the frostsliver's idea of a joke. An almost inaudible tinkle in her mind seemed to confirm it, and Sabira smiled in response.

The rubble of the main monastery squatted over the glacier, which still flowed from the bowels of the mountain, unimpeded by the tonnes of stone that had come down on it.

In bright daylight, Sabira could see that the destruction had not been total. The great entrance was not intact, but a dark crack was visible in the debris: a way in. Whatever had destroyed the ancient structure had started inside, for that was where the collapse was most severe.

Sabira hesitated before entering. She knew that this might be the last time she saw the sky.

She took one long look back to the rest of the Aderasti mountain range spiking up into the distance and to where, far away, the ash clouds of the huge Ignatian geysers rose, looking like the smoke of campfires from this distance.

There was more out there too. There were the plains nations, and other mountain ranges beyond them. Fanciful stories from Ignata said that, further away, there was a great sea that no one dared try to cross – but who knew for sure? The world was vast, and – she realized with regret – she would never see it all.

Even Tserah didn't see it all.

That thought brought Sabira down. It was the shadow of her fears, her worry that she might never return to the surface.

You have options. You could stay here, as Packman Mihnir suggested. Build a fire, signal for rescue.

'No,' said Sabira. 'There aren't any options. If we

148

stay here, the rescuers will never reach Mihnir in time. I won't leave him to die.'

If you're sure . . .

She touched the model ash-cat in her pocket, hoping it would bring her more luck than it had brought her brother. With a heavy heart, she turned away from the light and went on into shadow.

The glacier seemed to motion her along as she walked beside it, swallowed in the shadow of the ruined entrance. Sabira found a passageway near the centre. She assumed it must once have been flanked by giant statues of robed monks, because pieces of the monuments littered her way and made a space barely large enough for her to fit through. Giant feet poked from under the destruction, their huge, crumbling snow boots draped with the chipped hems of robes. Head bowed, Sabira picked her way past, feeling like an insect scuttling through a crack into a house.

The passage opened into a grand entry hall, where there were more broken corpses of sculptures and statues. At the hall's rear, wide steps that might have been scarlet sank deep into the mountain. Fallen rock and stonework had stemmed the staircase off entirely, centuries-old stone rent by some unnatural power. This wasn't time's work.

No. It wasn't.

Sabira stared at the blackened pattern of the blast

that had destroyed the stairs, smelt the acrid stench in the air. She knew that scent too well, though she had only known it once before. Hatred and horror built in her heart, along with understanding. She knew how it had happened.

This was where the destruction had started. Here, with the massive bang she had heard after she'd cut her frostsliver. She knew what had caused the avalanche. She knew why the monastery was strewn with recent rubbish. She knew for sure what she had only half suspected last night. It had not been the mountain that tried to kill her. It had been men – Ignatians – and their blasting powder.

They had beaten her mother, and scared Sabira half to death, and now they were here to finish the job. Her eyes stayed fixed on the rubble. Had they done that to seal the way behind them, or out of contempt for the sacred places of the Aderasti?

Either way, the Ignatians had to be down there, locked off by stone. She had almost put it together the last night, with the tracks and wreckage, but her tiredness had robbed her of certainty. What could they be doing? Surely nothing good.

Something lit within Sabira. Where she had been cold, resigned to her fate, now she felt hot anger, and she was not alone. The frostsliver burnt with rage against these people who had murdered its lifelong companion, Tserah.

'How dare they?' Sabira whispered. 'How dare you?' she yelled at the cold stone, the words echoing pointlessly.

They will pay. Together, we will make them.

Sabira breathed, and breathed, and tore her eyes from the evidence of the crime against her, and against her people.

To make this right, she had to solve the problem – how would she descend into the mountain, if not by the ruined stairs?

The glacier. Look.

Sabira looked. In the centre of the hall, the glacier boiled up from an enormous pit, like blood from a wound, before flowing out sideways in the direction she had entered.

The pit was ringed with stones, but Sabira guessed it was a natural formation, with the monastery built here because of it. When she craned over to look inside, she found the bottom was beyond sight, swallowed in blackness and drifting, thin vapour lit blue by the frostfire. It was like a horrible mouth, and Sabira had never seen anything more forbidding. No one in living memory had descended through the pit – but the legendary First Bonded had been here before the monastery or the stairs. They must have come this way. It must be possible.

The idea of climbing down the constantly-moving

glacier seemed terrifyingly stupid, but Sabira saw that she had no choice. The rope was coiled tight around her, over her shoulder and between her legs, and tied securely to a nearby rock. The frostsliver had helped her. Tserah had climbed a lot, in her time. It didn't feel safe, but the frostsliver assured her that if she kept a firm grip, it would be. If it wasn't, at least the horror would be short.

Do not think – just do.

Sabira nodded and backed towards the lip of the pit, hating every step. Then her boots touched the edge, and there was no more time for such thoughts. She was standing on a wall, and not plunging to her death after all.

Sabira held there for a moment. She wanted to stop, to remain a part of the surface world, but Aderast beckoned. The glacier moaned and cracked in encouragement, and Sabira took her first stride into the abyss.

For a handful of steps, Sabira was able to rappel down the rock with ease, before her feet met the moving surface of the glacier and she nearly slipped. A few seconds of near disaster passed, before she was on the wall of ice, treading slowly and going nowhere, as it tried to carry her back up. It was a weird sensation, but once she began letting out rope again, she felt steadier.

Looking back to check that she wasn't walking into any obstructions, Sabira dropped lower and lower, the rope playing through her trembling hands. She kept her pace slow and deliberate, not wanting to risk making a mistake and fatally releasing her braking grip. It soon became a frustrating experience, since she couldn't stop to rest, or the ice would carry her upwards, wasting her efforts. She sweated through her furs, heating up uncomfortably despite the cold darkness.

Not being able to use the frostsliver to assist made things a lot harder too – if it touched the glacier, it would be absorbed back into it. She was forced to rely only on the strength of her fingers on the rope. It caused hot friction as it ran across Sabira's gloves, so much that she worried it might burn into them.

Don't worry. Tserah used to do this all the time. She never set her clothes on fire.

Sabira smiled weakly and carried on down. As she settled into a careful, unpleasant rhythm the whole thing began to feel like a dream, what with the strange motion under her and the ever-present glow of the glacier. Below the surface, there was no snowfall to blanket it, and the eerie blueness of the ice was almost as clear as crystal. The glacier was the only light now, and its frostfire filled her vision with hypnotic intensity.

Several times, Sabira worried that the glacier's bulk would swell to take up the entire pit and cut off her way down, leaving her to be carried all the way back up the entire shaft.

Most bulges proved passable without too much effort, but one found her having to quickly shuffle all the way to one end of the pit to find a gap she could fit through. After an awkward wiggle, she squeezed past, her back scraping painfully against rock.

She would have felt relieved, except that she could see another ridge in the glacier coming up at her. She began sidling to one side, thinking that she would have to worm her way through again. She was right, but with another glance she saw that the only gap large enough for her was some distance away.

That didn't seem like a problem until she was moving to line up with it. Sabira felt the rope try to pull her back the way she had come, and almost let go in shock.

The rope above her was a straight diagonal back to the last ridge she had slotted through, and as the glacier ground past on its unstoppable way upwards, the line danced in her hand. Already too far committed, Sabira got in position and descended through the second hole.

A few more footfalls told her that there was no way for the rope to go back to vertical – it was going to stay taut between the two opposite points. She knew it was dangerous, but she could do nothing except hope that the rope held out until she reached the bottom, wherever that might be.

Then a tiny sound echoed down from above.

Uh-oh.

It was the sound of a trapped rope fraying and snapping. A slight vibration in the line was the last warning she got before the firm, comforting hold of the rappelling line went totally slack.

Sabira fell into darkness.

PART V

CHAPTER SIXTEEN

The ice water hit Sabira more than she it, the impact like being punched across half of her body at once. Thoughts burst from her head from the force of it and she went limp. Only several seconds later did her senses return.

She was underwater. Freezing. Drowning. Not knowing which way was up, Sabira floundered, her furs heavy with water.

The frostsliver chimed in alarm in Sabira's head. Her heart was beating like it was going to explode, trying to pump even a flicker of warmth around her veins.

She couldn't swim, really – for her, liquid usually came in nothing larger than a barrel. Sabira beat at the water, but the stuff was clawing. It wanted to take her to its depths and never let go. All she could do was fight. Pushing and pulling and kicking, somehow she battled her way to the shimmering, unreal surface.

Lungs burning, she ripped free of the water just long enough to swallow a tiny breath. Air had never seemed so precious or so hard to claim. In that moment, Sabira caught a glimpse of dark stone and water, lit by the glacier. And there, the rim where water met rock. Sanctuary.

She struggled and flailed her way across the pool, pushing aside chunks of ice and pulling herself through slush. She quickly lost all feeling in her limbs, and her splashing grew even less coordinated. Fighting to stay on the surface felt impossible with her boots, clothes and her pack doing everything they could to drag her down. She wanted to throw it all off, but without her supplies, she was dead anyway.

Finally, her arm touched the edge. The stone was slick and slippery, and she couldn't get purchase on it.

'Help!' Sabira gasped.

The frostsliver surged out through her glove, forming into giant predatory fingers, its claws long and sharp. She slammed it down, the nails cutting into the rock. Using its grip and power, she hauled herself free to flop on to the rock. It was cold here too, but like a cooking stove in comparison to the evil chill of the water.

There was almost no more strength in her arms, but still she dragged herself away from the edge of the pool, as if the water might rise and pull her back in. Seconds passed.

It was only now that Sabira began to feel how cold she was. Shivers wracked her body and her heart wouldn't stop hammering. Her breath was coming in rapid wheezes and her vision was blurry. She had escaped the water, but the cold might claim her life, even so.

This should help.

She felt the frostsliver flatten and spread across her skin, forming a thin barrier between her and the sodden clothing, as it had done when she'd been stranded in the snowstorm. It was relief like stepping into a warm bath, but Sabira was still chilled through. She stripped away her top layer of furs, squeezed out her dark hair and huddled by a rock wall to shiver until feeling and thought came back.

Sabira reached for the ash-cat in her pocket and held it. After a while, she found it easy to drift away, dozing a little, wonderfully free of dreams of any kind.

Sabira woke in the dark. She didn't know how much time had passed; in the cave there was no way to know. She was just happy not to have been found by any

Ignatian soldiers or yeti while she was asleep.

She opened her pack, and found that her supplies had mostly survived. Aderasti bags were made for harsh weather, and would keep out snow, sleet and rain. Going swimming with one was a different story, however, and the oiled lining had not kept all the water out.

She surveyed the damage. The food would dry out, though its taste would have suffered. Her firewood and firelighters might still be useful, but not any time soon. Her blankets, like her clothes, were damp but would also dry. The water skeins were intact. The pool had not killed her.

'Nothing to do except go on,' she said, and the frost-sliver tinged in agreement. Easier said than done. Every step in this place was one more towards Ignatians, or maybe a yeti. Sabira wasn't sure which was worse. Could the yeti she had seen have something to do with the Ignatian invasion? Was the mountain angry?

Sabira gazed at the glacier as it flowed upwards. She had no idea why it did that, and it felt strange to be so ignorant when a part of the thing was joined to her.

'I guess this is where you were . . . born, I suppose,' she found herself saying. 'Along with every other frost-sliver. How does that even work? Why does every slice of the glacier become a frostsliver?'

After a thoughtful silence, the frostsliver said,

I *am many of many. I am a legion with one voice.*

162

'What does that mean?'

I don't know. Things I once knew are cut off from me. Once I was a piece of a greater mind. I am still, but now there is a wall between me, and the rest of me. One day I may be one with the rest again, though I can't be sure. That frightens me. What if I never return – or what if I do and lose everything that Tserah helped me gain?

Sabira had no answer to that. Maybe no one did.

'Do you ever wish that Tserah had left you where you were?' she felt compelled to ask.

There was a short silence, then,

I would not be without her.

'But . . . you miss your . . . family?' Sabira guessed.

I can hear the voices of the others in the glacier. Or just an echo of them. Like someone is talking quietly a few rooms over. I know that I once knew them, and now . . . I have forgotten so much.

Sabira tried to imagine being locked away from her parents for ever, knowing that they were out there somewhere. It didn't exactly fit.

Your brother. It is as bad as your not knowing his fate.

Sabira froze. No other reminder could have chilled her so deeply. As with every time Kyran's memory came to her, guilt came rushing back. She gripped the ash-cat toy. She would never be able to say goodbye, or welcome him home again.

'I think we should get going,' she said abruptly. The memories were too much to talk about, even with one who shared her head.

All right.

After finding her way out of the cavern, Sabira spent hours following the stream of ice down into the mountain as best she could. In the stories about the First Bonded and the Deep Explorers, all had tracked the glacier to its source and found a way out to Adranna from the deeps – Sabira had to trust that, somehow, she would do the same.

It was difficult, though, when the glacier was prone to plunging through holes in the rock no wider than itself. Each time Sabira was forced to choose another route and hope to meet the Tears of Aderast further down in the silent dark. Every corner was a worry, but Sabira saw no sign of Ignatians and after a while some of the tension left her. Some.

Allow me to light the way.

Perhaps to raise her spirits, the frostsliver rippled to her hand, forming a kind of wide cylindrical lantern, suspended from her palm by strands of ice. It cast frostfire all around, helping her avoid tripping over her feet.

Soon, it began encouraging her, tinkling hints and feelings as to which passageway to take. Sometimes it took animal form to point a wing or paw, resembling a puppet on strings while it did so, and seemingly unworried about getting lost. It was all very well for it, sensing the presence of the glacier without sight.

I can sense the glacier's strength. I know where it is, and how deep we are.

That was slightly comforting, though only slightly.

The claustrophobic tunnels made Sabira yearn for some space to stretch, to walk freely, to run even, although she didn't have much energy for it. Instead, she mechanically crawled or slid or squeezed through cramped corridors and shafts into the next section and down to the next, finding it hard to believe that there was any way out.

Memories and fears ran through her head. Uncle Mihnir, dying in that desolate cave. A burning forest. A red-hot lash. Her mother's beaten face. The Ignatians were here to cause her people harm, Sabira knew it. But how?

'What's that?' Sabira said suddenly, spotting something on the floor of the gently sloped pit she was climbing down. A minute or so later when she had scrambled the rest of the distance, she saw that the glint belonged to a brass button. A button with a snarling ash-cat carved into its surface.

She was following in Ignatian footsteps.

Sabira rested. Ate. Slept fitfully. Continued. Over the following hours she encountered more evidence of life having been in the tunnels. A bone here and there. The remains of cookfires. Each find made her more fearful.

As she emerged into a larger cavern, she heard noises. Not the gentle, comforting cracks of the glacier, but something more animal, echoing down the tunnels. It might have been whispers, or howls far away. The underground space made it impossible to be sure.

Take care.

Sabira chose to assume the worst, dropping to the floor and lying flat, only allowing enough of her head to poke above the lip of her ledge in order to see.

As she did so, the frostsliver disappeared inside her clothes, leaving Sabira in almost complete darkness. Without its glow, she could see a light below coming from another tunnel across, and it was getting stronger. Not the bluish light of the glacier or the yeti but orange and flickering. Sabira moved no muscle, save for her pumping heart.

The dancing light lent long and confused shadows to the things that came out of it. Sabira made out four limbs and dark, leathery skin in the darkness. When one of the half-dozen figures turned slightly, she caught a glimpse of beady, black, glassy eyes looking out of a face overgrown by fur.

The smell of the burning oil wafted to Sabira's nostrils and with it something else. That oily stench wasn't only coming from the lantern they held, but from the walkers themselves.

Of course. Those weren't eyes at all, they were

crystal goggles. The strange fur and skin belonged to a long coat. Ignatians. Monsters of a different kind.

They infest Aderast. Defile it.

They were obviously at least a little prepared for the mountain, for they wore makeshift furs – but the clothes looked like they were designed by someone with only the vaguest idea of what proper cold weather garments should be. It explained the shivering – they must be half frozen.

The six Ignatians stopped in the middle of the cavern and laid down their burdens. Some had packs, all had muskets on their backs, and two at the rear carried a small barrel between them. Sabira did her best to breathe as quietly as possible as she watched, and hoped that her heart wasn't the snare drum it sounded like in her ears.

'By the lash, I'll be glad to get out of these creepy tunnels and back to the rest of the regiment. How much further are we from the camp?' the large Ignatian at the front of the group asked. So there was a whole camp of them. Soldiers. Maybe even an army housed in these dark caverns. What were they doing?

Look closer.

Sabira did, her eyes settling on the barrel to which the frostsliver was drawing her attention. It had a red symbol painted on it that evoked danger and things exploding.

Blasting powder.

Hatred for the stuff flowed through Sabira's veins, both her own feelings, and the frostsliver's too. Their combined anger made her want to leap the gap and attack, damn the consequences.

Except that would be suicide. Sabira stopped, checked herself and fixed the Ignatians with all of her attention. She couldn't fight them. She could listen, though, and plot.

'How much further?' the thickset leader demanded again. A thin, wiry figure, holding something that could be a piece of paper or leather, walked over, raising it up to the light.

'By my calculations,' he said, 'we've got another couple of days before we reach Adranna.'

Sabira narrowed her eyes. That voice was younger, and familiar somehow.

'You'd best not get it wrong. I don't want to be wandering these tunnels for the rest of my life.'

The larger man – who Sabira realized also seemed familiar – squinted at the calculations, but didn't seem to be making much of them.

'Wouldn't worry too much about not finding our way,' the wiry man helpfully supplied. 'We'll hear the blast when they break out of the mountain behind Adranna. Worst comes to worst we can follow that. Would have been better if we'd never had to split from the regiment in the first place, of course.'

The blast when they break out of the mountain . . .

Sabira's throat felt dry, her heart a fluttering thing in her chest. They were heading to Adranna too – and they intended to take it.

'We had to stay behind, conscript,' snapped the large man. 'Someone had to babysit you while you set the charges. Sealing the monastery was important. Don't want anyone following us in – or any cowardly deserters getting out.'

'That probably set off an avalanche, you know,' the wiry man said. Strangely, he did not sound happy about it. Where had she heard his voice before?

'Added benefit. They'll be busy dealing with it when we attack. Even less resistance – not that there would have been much anyway.'

'What if we need to retreat?' another of the men interjected. He was older, his hair starting to grey.

'With a thousand muskets on our side? By the lash, those Aderasti barely manage to make bows, and they won't be expecting us. If there are any casualties at all, I'll be surprised.'

'Besides the ones that died already, you mean,' said the thin one, without humour.

'They were weak,' the leader snapped, as callous as Sabira had come to expect from Ignatians.

'Oh, I'm sure that those monsters that took Henlo would have backed off if he'd been just a little tougher,' the thin man said sullenly. Apparently, this was a step too far for his leader, as he stalked up to the soldier with aggression clear even in the low light.

'Do you want to taste the branding lash again?' he demanded, and Sabira stifled a squeak of fear, both at the comment, and at the glint of silver on the man's shoulder. She recognized him now – and the burnt rip in his mouth. A tremble started in her hands, and she could do nothing to stop it. The young soldier seemed to see a little of the danger, but by his defiant tone, not nearly enough of it.

'I'd rather not even see it again, if you don't mind,' he said.

'That's, "If you don't mind, Sergeant Major Lifan" to you, and if you want that, you'd best keep in line.'

It sounded like good advice to Sabira, but the smaller man did not seem to agree.

'Well, Sergeant Major Lifan,' the younger man said, seemingly without the sense to know when to be quiet, 'can I pretty please not see it again?'

The sergeant major's fist caught him in the stomach the moment the last word passed his lips. It seemed that punishment was swift in the Ignatian army. As the soldier crumpled to the floor, Lifan called,

'We're resting here for a bit. Break out the rations.'

Sabira held as still as she could while the Ignatians found places to sit and began taking rations from their packs. Fortunately, none of them looked up – or if they did glance in her direction, the shadows of the cave hid her from sight.

Most of the men chose positions in the centre of the room, but the younger man, helped by the greying one, made his way to a spot under Sabira's ledge. Maybe they wanted to be away from Lifan, but she wished they had picked somewhere else.

The two of them ate their meals and it was a minute or two before either said anything. Sabira was starting to think that they wouldn't, when the older one broke the silence.

'You need to learn when to shut that trap of yours, Danlin,' he said, then added, 'You know, if you commit to this life, you can make something out of it.'

'In between dropping avalanches on civilians and burning a bunch of old books no one was ever going to read, just because of Lifan's spite.'

The older man sighed.

'Don't you have any national pride? Ignata is going to be covered in glory for years after this.'

'So I heard when the recruiters came knocking,' said the young man. 'See the world, they said. Meet new people and kill them, they said. No, I said, and they hit me with a cudgel. Woke up on my way to this ice hole.'

'Look at it this way, it could be worse.'

'How?' the younger soldier said.

'At least we get to be patriotic, claiming back the lands of our ancestors and all that.'

The younger one grunted derisively and said, 'You think I care? The officers are all fanatics – they think

171

they're on some grand mission to avenge past wrongs. The Aderasti can keep their pretty magic trinkets.'

Trinkets?

The frostsliver seethed. Sabira frowned. Maybe they weren't all bloodthirsty zealots, then. The thought ought to have made Sabira feel better, but it didn't. The older man sighed at his companion, and began to explain slowly, like adults did when they thought you didn't know what you were talking about.

'Look, you're a colonies boy, right? You don't know what it's like in Ignata proper. The ash geysers are worse every year now. Harvest is barely surviving.'

'I thought the ash fertilized good crops?' the young man said.

'Maybe a few generations ago! The ash fall's heavier these days, and too much of a good thing can be deadly. There won't be enough food to go round when our sons and daughters are grown. There are a lot of farmers scratching around in the ash who look up at the mountains with envy. Clear air, fertile ground on the lower slopes, security from raiders in the towns and cities, and magic at the peak.'

'So?'

'There are a lot who say that, in the days of the old empire, when Ignata controlled the mountains, the ash geysers were commanded by magic. Some think that the frostslivers might be the thing we need to be great again. So they say we need more land, and we need frostslivers. It's a matter of survival.'

'If you say so,' the young soldier said. 'Not sure I want a monster poking around in my head.'

'The officers may not give you much choice.'

Sabira's attention, already rapt, focused in on that piece of information like a hawk. What were the Ignatians intending to do? Apparently she was not the only one curious, as the young man asked,

'Has anyone tried to bond with one?'

'They had someone try. Didn't work out. I figure they must want to get an Aderasti to tell them how to do it without killing more of us.'

Sabira hoped that frostslivers could not be fooled into a bonding – but what if they could? If she were caught and forced to reveal what she knew about bonding, the Ignatians might have hundreds of bonded frostslivers at their command on top of their army.

As she lay on her ledge watching, Sabira's will turned to iron. She needed that strength, for as the two men fell silent, eating their food, Sabira realized with a chill that the fate of Adranna had settled on to her shoulders.

CHAPTER SEVENTEEN

Following the Ignatians felt less like a sensible plan with every hour, but Sabira could see no way round it. They were moving in the same direction after all. Down into the mountain, tracking the course of the glacier.

We cannot lose them.

The frostsliver kept telling her so, but Sabira knew it all too well. There was no escape from the constant tension. What if they discovered her? The man with the whip would brand her, and probably kill her. She couldn't think like that, she knew, but awful possibilities kept occurring to her. She concentrated on her feet, and on not making a scrap of noise, moving only when she was sure that the Ignatians had moved on far enough for it to be safe.

The continuous concentration and fear began to take its toll as the minutes – or hours – dripped by, her path lit by the dim glacier light. Every time she caught a snatch of conversation, Sabira had to fight not to jump out of her skin.

'I'm freezing,' was a common refrain, as were swear words, and curses against Aderast. Through it all she remained a panicked shadow. Fortunately, the mountain granted them an easy path, the passages broadening and slanting gradually downhill.

'Well, guess we know which way we're going,' said the young soldier, not far ahead.

'Now that I can agree with, conscript.'

Lifan. Sabira crept closer. If they were making a choice about which way to go, she needed to know what they decided. The group were standing at the end of a wide cavern peppered with a handful of tunnel mouths. Most of the passages were small, and lit dull blue by clumps of luminous fungi. The one the Ignatians picked was wide, straight and clear. The glacier was flowing out of it.

Sabira waited a spell until the sounds of the soldiers' boots had faded, then ventured out. The passage they had chosen, lit brighter than the others by the frostfire, angled down slightly and didn't seem to bend in the slightest.

She couldn't follow, she realized. They'd spot her with a single glance back.

'Keep an eye out for those creatures. Don't let any sneak up on us,' she heard the sergeant major say distantly. Well, that settled it.

'They're following the glacier, and you can always lead us back to it, right?' Sabira silently said to the frostsliver.

Probably.

That would have to do. She stepped down a tunnel that seemed to be heading in a similar direction, her path lit by blue fungal lights.

The tunnel split again and again, and Sabira feared she had walked into a maze. The frostsliver's senses steered Sabira through the winding passages, eventually leading her to a flat rock wall. A dead end? No. There was a tiny hole in the base of the wall, barely wide enough for her shoulders. Nothing she had passed through had been so small, and the idea of fitting into it filled her with dread.

'Seriously?' she whispered. 'Isn't there another way?'

I think this is the only way forward. It's not like I want to risk our lives.

She decided to face the challenge after getting a meal into her – her insides had been protesting for a while.

Sabira looked through her pack for something appetizing and found few choices. Her meat was mostly gone, and she had only one pastry left. It hadn't come through its soaking well, and flopped wetly when she unwrapped it.

She ate it despite its condition, picking over the rest as she chewed. There would only be a day or so of food left. That might be stretched a bit further, but not much. If she got desperate, there were always the mysterious meat scraps that she had scavenged from the monastery ruins. Of course, even if they did not poison her, they were not much of a meal.

'I'll probably be out of food before we get there,' she mused aloud, and with a pang realized that it would be the same for Mihnir. She pushed thoughts of her uncle away – she couldn't help him, not until she got out. She was only barely getting by herself.

You are doing as well as could be expected.

It sounded almost impressed.

'If you say so,' she said, then washed her food down with the last of one of the water skeins, before looking again at the evil hole in the base of the wall. It was waiting for her. Best to get it over with.

The space was only just large enough for her to fit into, with no guarantee that she would make it all the way through. There was no room to keep her pack on her back. Sabira took it off and tied it to her foot with a length of rope so she could pull it after her.

She ran her tongue across her lips, trying to think of a way to trick herself into believing that this would turn out well. Suddenly the light changed, shadows dancing towards her from where she had come.

Hide! I sense them!

The frostsliver's chime was a panicked alarm. Sabira whirled around, her heart racing – there was nowhere to hide.

Sabira almost wished that the frostfire would vanish, leaving her veiled in darkness. Then she wouldn't have been able to see the monsters, and more importantly, they would not be able to see her.

There were three of them at the mouth of her dead-end passage, and each turned inhumanly blank eyes towards Sabira, faces encased in living ice and softly glowing with menace. Yeti.

They were like the creature she had seen among the ruins, and this time she could be sure they were real. Each was vaguely the shape of a person, but that was the only similarity. The things had no neck, but still towered at least three heads taller than Sabira, like cliffs of malevolent ice. Small icicle spikes jutted from their luminescent blue skin at random, making them look even bigger. The creatures' feet and hands were oversized, even compared to the bulk of the rest of their bodies, and the bodies were misshapen, like clay figurines made by a mitten-wearing child.

These must have been the 'creatures' that killed that

soldier the young Ignatian had mentioned. What should she do?

We have to go!

She would run, but there was nowhere to go. One of the yeti moved towards her in a strange, shambling gait, giving Sabira no chance to think, no chance to do anything but feel sick terror rising in her throat.

There was no roar or bone-chilling scream as the creature stomped slowly down the narrow passage, but the heavy thuds of its ice feet were just as scary.

What did it want? To kill her? To eat her?

Sabira scrambled backwards awkwardly, fumbling across the stone and doing everything she could to buy more distance from the creature as it awkwardly stomped towards her. It was no use – the thing had her trapped.

Sabira felt the frostsliver slithering down her arm, but knew that not even its magic could help her. She held up her hands in a feeble defence as the yeti came at her, its paw raised, and saw the frostsliver flow through her glove, expanding into a thin, icy shield.

It wouldn't be enough. It couldn't be. However strong a frostsliver might be, that thing looked like it could smash through solid rock. Sabira braced herself for an impact – but impossibly, the yeti was slowing down. Stopping. Sabira peered at it, heart thundering, as it looked at the shield curiously, examining it.

A memory came to her of how her mother dealt

with dangerous animals, making noise and waving arms in an attempt to confuse them.

Sabira, I don't think . . .

'Get away!' Sabira yelled. 'Get back! I mean it!'

It was ridiculous – but the yeti's paw snapped back as if it had been burnt. Astonished, Sabira didn't know how to react. All she could do was stare with wide eyes and wait for the creature to overcome its surprise and strike. The blow did not come.

She wondered for an instant if the creature really had been scared off by the appearance of strength, but the yeti hadn't quite backed off – it had just stopped reaching out.

'Please,' she begged. 'Just leave me be.'

The giant creature retreated a step or two. It stood motionless, its blank face staring at her.

Sabira sensed something in that look – she couldn't say what, but there was more meaning there than an animal could normally share. She seized upon the thing's confusion, or whatever else had come upon it, knowing that there might be no other chance to make her escape.

Turning, she pulled in the frostsliver shield and dove arms first into the hole, wriggling into the tight space as fast as possible. Too late she had the horrifying thought that the yeti might pull her back by the rope binding her pack to her leg. She pushed forward frantically, hoping the creature wasn't that smart.

Push! Push! You can do this!

The space was like an animal's gullet, and she the willing prey heading into its belly. It was far too small to turn around in, and the slight downward curve made it impossible to do anything but crawl slowly onwards. She couldn't go back, even if she wanted to.

As her mind touched that last dreaded thought, her glove touched something much worse. Heart leaping into her mouth, Sabira swept her arm back and forth.

Freezing water was everywhere, filling the tiny tunnel, and there was nowhere to go except into it head first. She reached in with an arm, desperately praying to feel dry stone on the other side, and finding none. That was almost enough to break her, but for the fact that her hand could feel the tunnel sloping gently upwards. That had to mean that there would be air soon after, didn't it?

We must go on. You can get us through.

Curse the frostsliver's cold logic. Slowly, she sank into the water. Arms, then head, neck, shoulders, waist and finally her legs, before she was fully immersed and pushing past the bend. Every instinct in her pushed Sabira to fight her way clear, though she could do nothing besides painstakingly drag herself, the frostsliver whispering in her mind,

A little further.

She fully rounded the bottom. She was not yet clear of the water. The slope up was slight, and the way out seemed infinitely longer than the way in. The air inside her already felt stale, and with no end in sight through the dark water, Sabira began to panic. She was going to drown here, her body never to be found.

Then she felt her hand splash out into air, and a flicker of hope cut in. She pushed forward, but too fast. Her body jammed at a particularly tight point and, eyes bulging, Sabira screamed inside her head. She fought and struggled, her seconds ticking away.

With one last wrench, her shoulders dislodged in a moment of sweet pain, and she was moving again. She cracked her head on the roof in her hurry and bubbles escaped her mouth, the awful sensation of water rushing to replace them.

Then her face was above the water, her head spinning with dizziness. What did that matter, though, when delicious air was hers once again? It turned out to matter a little, as she crawled out of the terrible trap and began to recover from the thrill of escaping death. Her lungs were on fire, and her eyes were not much better. Water had got into everything it shouldn't, and her body was bumped and bruised.

Gasping and spluttering water between breaths, Sabira curled into a ball on the floor, her drenched clothing dripping on to the stone.

We cannot stay like this.

She knew it, but resented being told so.

Reluctantly, Sabira sat up and pulled the pack

through the narrow passage, glaring at it as it popped up above water, jealous of how easy its trip had been. She pulled it on to dry ground and started to untie the bag, interrupted by a fit of coughing that brought up more water. Somewhere towards the end, the coughs turned to sobs, and she had to fight the instinct to cry. The frostsliver stayed silent as she beat her emotions into submission. What could it say, when every hour down here seemed more hopeless, with something worse in store for her? Sabira tried to remember that each one brought her closer to Adranna. To home. But it was hard.

She laid out her furs to dry, shivering as the frostsliver again spread across her skin to keep her warm. It wasn't working very well.

Our bonding did not go as well as it could have. My abilities were stronger with Tserah.

That did not make Sabira feel better. In fact, she could feel everything welling up inside. The stress, the fear, the fatigue overflowed, and the strength leaked from her limbs.

She rubbed at her face and eyes, trying to clear the panic and terror from her system. Every time something else happened it seemed to burrow further into her. Would it ever leave, even if she made it home?

Sabira felt in her pocket for the ash-cat talisman, and found to her dismay that it wasn't there. She ran her eyes across the ground. Nothing. She must have lost it in the water – or maybe even before. It was gone, and with it her only memento of her brother.

Slumping to one side, her shoulder meeting the cave wall, Sabira whispered,

'I can't keep doing this,'

It was all too much. She slid to the floor, giving in to the pull of her feelings.

You can.

'Something will get me in the end. I can't keep being lucky.'

The agony was in the expectation. Sabira knew that it was coming, just not how. Would it be a fall? A monster? Shot by a soldier? Perhaps madness would take her, if she were stuck in the dark long enough.

We've come this far. Further than I could've believed.

'Maybe I deserve this place,' she said quietly. She felt a cold anger wash over her through the bond. The frostsliver wanted her to know that it opposed that idea. To drive the point home, it added aloud,

Tserah chose you. You are strong.

Sabira didn't answer.

Get up.

The frostsliver's patience was fraying. Sabira didn't move.

Get up now! I will let you have no peace until you do.

Really?

Up! Up! Up! Up! Up!

'All right!'

Sabira found herself on her feet, emotions confused. Her despair was edged with anger now, at the frostsliver, at the mountain, at her own weakness. Though she was still tired and cold, her freezing up seemed somehow silly. She wasn't sure if she wanted to cry or scream, and the war between the two meant that neither came.

Slowly, all of it faded to a dull ache.

I'm sorry.

'No,' Sabira replied. 'I'm sorry I needed it.'

That didn't mean that everything was all right. She had needed to escape that emotional hole, but physically Sabira was drained. She was ready to collapse, and would have if the idea hadn't felt like failure. Then she looked up and saw frostfire glowing nearby, subtle but clear on the stone.

Sabira grabbed her things and stumbled around the corner into a wide passageway, where the glacier greeted her with its blue glow. She noticed again how it seemed brighter down here than on the surface, purer almost – like the dance of actual firelight. There was not an Ignatian in sight. Her path had been twisty and this passage was direct. Perhaps they had already gone past.

She almost didn't care one way or the other. She was safe again – for the moment.

Sabira!

The jolt of alarm through the bond shot Sabira to

alertness. The frostsliver had heard something through her ears – the soft tramp of feet.

The Ignatians had not gone past.

They were coming now.

CHAPTER EIGHTEEN

Sabira ducked into the side passage, and not a moment too soon.

Lantern light illuminated the area, and Sabira stayed very still as the booted footsteps approached closer and closer. As the light brightened, it became more difficult to control her quickening pulse.

She couldn't get away – the only retreat was back through the drowning hole to the yeti, and even Ignatians didn't seem worse than that. Couldn't they hurry up and go past?

'Halt!'

Lifan's shout, steps away from her hiding place, was

loud enough to make Sabira jump. She held her breath as she heard the rest gather next to their leader.

'Are you sure this is right?' the sergeant major demanded. 'I don't like it. Keep seeing shadows – and there isn't any sign of the regiment.'

'They're probably still a day ahead of us,' the young soldier who had been navigating said. 'And, yes, I'm sure.'

'How?' his superior demanded.

'All we have to do is follow the glacier down to the correct altitude, which is what the regiment was doing, and it's been getting easier the further we go. Anyone with a mind can see that.'

Sabira could have told him not to say that, but from the sound of pain he let out, the soldier had already discovered it for himself.

'I'm about done with you, conscript. It's time you learnt a lesson,' Lifan announced. 'We'll go ahead, and you can find your own way back. Let's see how confident you are then. I don't want to see your face again before we get back – *if* you get back. Maybe if you can manage that, I'll forget about giving you another lick of the branding lash. Maybe. Or maybe the yeti will eat you, we'll see.'

None of the other Ignatians argued, not even the older man who had sat with the conscript before. Sabira listened as they moved off, and a while later the steps of the younger soldier followed at a slow trudge.

An idea came to Sabira, a terrible one that she saw no way round. She needed to know what the Ignatians knew, exactly what they planned, and here was one alone and as vulnerable as anyone holding a musket could be.

You want to capture and question an armed soldier? This seems ... unwise.

It did sound silly, she had to admit. However young, the conscript was a grown man, a trained fighter. She was one girl, tired, injured and unarmed save for the frostsliver. But she had to know what they were doing here, and this was her chance. She wasn't going to get a better one.

For once, the mountain had provided the answer, not the problem. Sabira remembered the snow-spine stinger. She had brought it all this way in the hope that it might be valuable to someone when she got home. It was going to be valuable much sooner.

She silently unpacked it from its place in the healer's kit. The water hadn't got inside, so it was as pristine as when she had lopped it off its owner on the mountain-side, if slightly desiccated. The venom should be just fine, though – she knew from her father that it stayed potent.

Sabira gently squeezed a drop from the sac, allowing it to bead on the tip of the stinger. Any more than that might permanently paralyse. In a way, that wasn't entirely unappealing. The frostsliver in particular didn't seem to care. In fact, Sabira thought she caught a hint of enthusiasm from it.

They destroyed the entrance to the mountain. Nearly killed us. Did kill Tserah. Remember.

'He has to be able to talk,' Sabira told it, slightly disturbed by the feelings that were coming through the bond, 'or what's the point?'

She didn't want to give in to that kind of feeling. She had seen what happened when people did. Burning forests. Red-hot lashes.

This will not be without blood. Even if Adranna is warned, there will still be war.

Sabira did her best to ignore these words as she ducked out of her recess and, worried that she might lose her prey, quickly padded after the soldier's lantern glow. Not as quickly as she would have liked – her knee was still stiffened by the frostsliver's numbing chill.

'I need my leg back,' she told the frostsliver mentally, and pain flared in her knee. The spike of agony only faded when the brace once more took up the strain.

Just . . . be careful. For both of our sakes.

Heart pounding, Sabira pushed on towards the soldier, stinger clutched firmly in hand. She had surprise on her side, but this could go wrong with the slightest mistake.

Sabira crept closer, staying by the cave wall where

she might just hope to be mistaken for a shadow if he turned. She got within a few strides of the soldier, close enough that she could see the light glinting off the metal barrel of his musket.

Then her boot tapped a pebble, sending it skittering across the ground, and Sabira's heart almost stopped. It would have been the end of her, had she frozen.

I am with you! Go!

She darted forward as the soldier began to turn, the magical brace on her leg pushing her into a powerful leap. As she flew towards him, she turned the stinger under the young soldier's hood and nicked his neck with the poisoned point. Instantly, he stiffened, his muscles locking as the venom coursed into him. He began to topple over a heartbeat later.

It was almost comical, but since he was about to hit the ground too hard to be funny, Sabira swept in and caught as much of his weight as she could manage without accidentally sticking him with the stinger a second time. His lantern clattered to the ground first, its glass smashing and light sputtering out, and Sabira winced at the sound.

As soon as he was on the ground, Sabira grabbed the soldier's hood, and dragged him away down a side passage. The others probably wouldn't come searching, but best not to risk it.

It was lucky that he was so slight, for Sabira found it

difficult to haul him along even as it was. She gave up as soon as they were out of sight of the main tunnel. Though her muscles quivered with adrenaline, Sabira had to smile. She'd done it.

Sabira knelt next to her captive and pulled his hood and goggles back, exposing a typical Ignatian face, though one that looked gaunt and thin. Now that Sabira was able to look closer, she saw that he was even younger than she had thought. This soldier couldn't be more than eighteen. Maybe less.

Do not let that fool you.

She nodded as he stirred a little, and tried to ready herself, hoping that she and the frostsliver were now in agreement. The frostsliver gave her its answer by numbing her knee again and growing into the shape of a hunting knife in her hand. Sabira moved closer to the soldier, watchful for any surprises. He shouldn't be able to move for a while, but Sabira wasn't taking any chances. Hopefully the dosage would let him speak, or this was going to be awkward.

The Ignatian's eyelids flickered open, and the instant that they did, she moved the frostsliver knife to his throat, attempting to appear threatening. As she did so, his dark eyes widened and words cracked his lips open.

'Aderasti . . .' he said, his frightened eyes reflecting frostfire from her glowing knife.

Sabira did her best not to betray how unsure of

herself she was, gripping her weapon tighter and inching it closer.

'Just remember, I could kill you right now,' she said.

'You're not going to kill me.'

Sabira wasn't sure how he could know that. She certainly didn't, and the frostsliver didn't have any qualms about the idea.

Only if he twitches wrongly.

'What have you done to me?' he asked.

The last bit had some fear in it. What was it about him that seemed so familiar?

'It'll wear off eventually,' Sabira answered, and on impulse added, 'If I let it.'

She took a moment to think about what she wanted to say next, going through possible ways to inspire fear. Each sounded silly in her head.

'Wait,' the boy said. 'I know you. You were there when Yupin burnt the forest.'

'What?' Sabira said, stunned.

'I said that he'd let you go if you didn't fight him. I'm sorry. I didn't know he'd have us fire volleys at you.'

Sabira's hand tightened around the frostsliver dagger. He wasn't lying – now he'd said it, she did recognize him. That was where she had heard his voice before, though she only half remembered it now. He had set the blasting powder that brought the avalanche down, but he hadn't wanted to. He had been there at the forest, one of the monsters who hurt her mother.

Maimed Kyran. Except he hadn't done the hurting.

'I'm going to save my people,' she said grimly, choosing not to respond to his words, 'and you're going to help me.'

'Why?'

She wracked her brain for something that she could offer. Certainly not money or power, but there might be something more valuable.

'Escape?' she suggested. It hadn't sounded like he wanted to be here.

'How're you going to manage that?' he croaked. That was good – he hadn't dismissed the idea.

He may be playing for time.

Sabira silently agreed that it was worth being wary. Still, this was promising.

'If you helped me, Adranna would welcome you,' she said. 'You could be free of the army.'

'You've been listening for a while, haven't you?' her prisoner replied.

'I heard enough.'

'Then you know how many of us are coming for your city. Adranna is not going to be a safe place for me, or you, or anyone soon.'

Sabira moved the dagger away from her captive and sat down next to him. It was clear that threats were pointless. She tried a different tack.

'It didn't sound like you all want to be doing this,' she said. 'I think maybe you're one of those who don't.

Why don't you tell me exactly what we're facing – and how to find them, and what their plans are?'

He gave a quiet, humourless laugh before answering.

'There are a thousand men in the regiment, as if it will help you – and I think you can guess what they intend to do.'

Nothing good.

'Humour me,' Sabira said, needing to be sure.

'You think it'll matter? They tell us that Aderasti can't fight, and I'm guessing there's some truth to it. We have lots of muskets, and you have none. Even your frostslivers won't beat that. Your ice walls will be useless – the army isn't going to go near them. In a few days, they'll blast out of the mountain behind the walls, into the city itself.'

His strength had come back a little, and his words were no longer so weak. Sabira thought she heard a note of, what, defiance, in them? This was a man who understood the power his people wielded, even if he didn't like it. Did that mean that he stood with them, or did it make him oppose them all the more?

'You're wondering how you can trust a word I tell you,' he said, reading her thoughts. 'I would too, but if you think I might be lying for them, look at my back. You'll see how much love I have for the Ignatian army.'

Sabira didn't understand, but she pushed him into a sitting position all the same, not bothering to be all that gentle. With the kind of brusque efficiency that her father always used with patients, she pulled up the soldier's coat, and the shirt beneath, exposing the skin of his back.

She gasped at the sight. She had heard the other soldiers say that this young man had tasted the branding lash, but she had not understood the full reality of what that meant. The lash had left his back a horrible mess of burn scars. No, it was worse than that.

They were not just burns, but letters. Each segment of that metal whip had to be a different symbol. It was the most evil kind of pen Sabira could imagine. Of course, she couldn't recognize the words, but that didn't make it less horrific.

'The first one says, "conscript",' explained the young soldier. 'The next is, "troublemaker", the third, "thief". The fourth says, "coward" – I got it because I didn't fire at you and your mother with the rest. They give you the first one on the day they write your name in the ledger. The volunteers, like Lifan, get a different one – and claim they're proud of it, but I guess they would, wouldn't they?'

He could be lying. Trying to gain your trust.

It was possible.

'Yupin had those brands under his eyes,' said Sabira slowly. 'He seemed pretty committed to the cause.'

The soldier nodded.

'Some zealots have it done to themselves. Ember-priests, and the people that follow them, like Colonel

196

Yupin. Faith and duty, Yupin says. It's about showing their belief. They think it doesn't count unless it's written by the lash.' He saw the revulsion in her face and quickly added, 'Not all of us believe in those stupid superstitions. We're not all like him.'

Sabira stiffened at hearing confirmation that Yupin was somewhere in these caverns. She'd guessed, but knowing made it so much worse. She continued, trying to keep the fear out of her voice,

'Then why hasn't anyone stopped him from attacking Adranna?'

'The judge who was supposed to be in charge of this mission tried when she discovered her diplomatic delegation had been turned into an invasion. Once they left Adranna, Yupin beat her bloody, branded her a coward, and took her prisoner, along with anyone who supported her. Not many thought about speaking up after that.' He bowed his head. 'If I was anything, I'd have tried – but it would have just earned more brands. I wouldn't have followed the army down here if I'd had a choice.'

Judge Meihu. She'd been in Adranna only days ago, an obstacle between the colonel and his fanaticism. It didn't sound like there had been much resistance to his removing it. That was the power of fear, dividing any opposition. This soldier might have resisted if others had, but alone he could do nothing.

Sabira looked at the man – or boy – trying to find

some sure sign he could be trusted. She could see one of his fingers twitching. The snow-spine venom wouldn't last for ever. She had to make up her mind.

Meeting his bright eyes for a few long seconds, Sabira said, 'But you do have a choice – now.'

She went to her pack and extracted the flask she had found at the monastery. Still mostly full, she thought it might make a good peace offering. She unscrewed it, prepared her tongue for the fiery taste and took a swig.

Urrgh. I am connected to your senses, remember?

'Who are you anyway? What's your name?' she asked, ignoring the frostsliver's complaint and putting the flask to the soldier's lips while hoping the burning sensation in her throat would go away soon.

'Danlin, former chemic apprentice, now a faceless conscript of the mighty Ignatian army,' he said, accepting a dose of the dark liquid with a smile.

'Well, faceless conscript, I'm Sabira, and together we're going to find a way to stop that mighty army of yours in its tracks.'

CHAPTER NINETEEN

Sabira and Danlin navigated the mountain's passages for hours, Danlin always trudging, crawling, or climbing ahead of her.

'It's times like these I miss home,' Danlin said. 'Not a single tunnel there, and blue-ish skies besides. Not so many things wanting to eat me either. Or stab me. Or shoot me. Shouldn't have left.'

Sabira had relieved him of his musket and carried it as she followed him down the tunnel, though she hated even touching the weapon. It wasn't entirely clear to her how the thing worked, but she'd seen crossbows before, and hoped not only that it was similar, but also that she wouldn't need to find out.

'You know, even with my musket, I don't think you'll be able to take on an army by yourself,' commented Danlin. 'And I doubt you can use that poison stuff on everyone – what was that anyway? I had blurred vision for ages – and I think my toes are still tingling.'

He talked a lot, often not expecting a reply.

'Guess your recruiters got you early too, then. You must be what, fifteen, sixteen?' Danlin said, glancing over his shoulder to check. 'You look a bit young to be fighting a war.'

Like he could talk.

'We don't have recruiters,' she replied, but before she could say more, he continued,

'What's it like having one of those frostslivers? Does it tell you what to do? I've heard you people think frostslivers are gods.'

The frostsliver chimed in amusement, liking the idea.

Yes – worship me!

Danlin jumped at the noise and turned to stare.

Sabira shook her head, smirking. 'Go on,' she said. 'We have to hurry.'

A minute later, they came to another open cavern, rimmed with a dozen other passageways. The way forward wasn't obvious, and Danlin stopped in the centre to cast his eye over the rough stone. Sabira

200

didn't spot any real difference between the first few, and Danlin bypassed each before coming to a passage lit by the glow of blue fungi. Sabira sucked in a breath at the sight of them, remembering the last time she'd noticed lots of the strange glowing fungus – she'd seen the yeti soon afterwards.

'Not that way,' she said, getting the frostsliver to slide into her hand and form a little yeti, by way of explanation. Danlin gaped at it, and then nodded.

'Wouldn't dream of it,' he said. 'Those things seem to like these mushrooms.'

Try that path – the one with the boulder.

It pointed a tiny yeti paw, and she followed the frostsliver's suggestion.

'The camp won't be much further down,' Danlin called back to her, reaching the bottom of a shaft. 'Assuming they managed to keep to schedule.'

'I don't want to walk straight into them,' Sabira said. 'I need to find somewhere to take a look without being spotted.'

'These caverns are riddled with passages and outcroppings. I'm sure that's possible if we're careful.'

Several times they almost stumbled into a patrol of soldiers, and every time Sabira half expected Danlin to cry out to them for rescue – but he didn't. Eventually, they found a crack of light in a passage wall and pushed through to a ledge above the biggest cavern Sabira had yet seen; it was lit with the flicker of flame.

'You've been good so far,' said Sabira. 'Don't wreck that now.'

She tapped the musket, and the soldier nodded in reply, with none of his usual chatter. Quickly, she and Danlin settled on to their bellies and edged forward, right up to the rock lip before peering over.

Lanterns had been pinned to the walls and fires burnt on the floor, fouling the air and lighting the cave walls in harsh yellowish colours that Sabira had barely seen in days. The Ignatians had made camp right next to the glacier. Finding it again should have been good news, but here its frostfire fought with the blazes next to it, and was of no comfort.

In this cavern alone there had to be a hundred men sitting around their campfires, and other fires shone in the multitude of passages beyond. A thousand soldiers. Sabira clenched her fists so hard she started to tremble.

They will pay. We will find a way to make them pay.

This must have been the colonel's plan all along, even as he and the other Ignatians came to Adranna as envoys for peace. That army that had come with him – the one her mother had thought a show of force – was an invasion. The moment the talks had failed – and how could they not, with Yupin involved? – they had only pretended to leave, and instead started up the mountain to find the secret way through it. Perhaps Yupin's Aderasti mother had told him the old stories too. Sabira wanted to scream. How could they betray the Aderasti like this?

'Are you all right?' Danlin whispered.

Sabira looked at him, nodded slowly. He hadn't asked for this, any more than she had. What would she have done in his place, forced to fight under threat of torture or death? She was glad not to know the answer.

'Even if I warn them . . . I'm not sure Adranna will be able to defend itself,' said Sabira softly, letting the realization sink in.

Danlin looked at her grimly. He had known that all along.

The city's inaccessibility was its best defence, not strength in numbers. These soldiers would break out from the rock face at the city's back and swarm across her home before defenders could respond. Adranna was doomed.

I will not believe that.

Sabira focused on the assembly below, hoping to see something that might prove her wrong. Instead, her eyes found the people in the crowd that scared her most. Yupin, wearing a flame-coloured ribbon of a stole with white and black stones wired in, like fresh and fire-spent coals. It didn't look part of his uniform – none of the other soldiers wore one.

He stood near the glacier with Lifan at his side, lit half in frozen blue and half in flickering orange. He looked almost like he was about to begin preaching, with Lifan there to scourge unbelievers. The sergeant major's branding lash hung at his side, the metal a cold grey, but the sight was frightening all the same.

The two monsters were standing waiting for the one woman in the Ignatian ranks. Her clothes were different from the soldiers too, more ceremonial than practical.

It had to be Judge Meihu, heading straight for the colonel and his minion, her garments tattered, long grey hair a mess, face abused.

She was being dragged through the crowd by a pair of soldiers, and not gently. Meihu didn't even look up when they forced her to her knees in front of Yupin and the sliding glacier. She seemed broken.

The judge's glove was yanked free, exposing flesh to the cold air, and she cried out in fear. For a moment, Sabira didn't understand what was going on, but then the guards began to manhandle the woman past their colonel, holding her naked hand towards the glowing blue ice.

No. They cannot!

Sabira stifled a gasp. They were going to force her to bond with the glacier. That was beyond wrong, it was vile. Gripping the rock she lay on, Sabira did everything she could not to let her anger boil over. She wanted to break something. The frostsliver felt precisely the same, enraged that its larger whole was being used like this.

'Anything to say for yourself, Judge?' Yupin asked, his voice ringing out.

Meihu did, sounding defiant, but scared. 'This is madness. Just because the ember-priests have said you can wear their stole now, doesn't make their ideas any more true. The judiciary still rules in Ignata, not the military, and certainly not some nonsense religion, whatever privileged place it may enjoy. The law . . .'

Yupin was no longer listening, if he'd ever started.

'Law is your luxury. My mother died coughing up her lungs, so full they were of ash. That is what drives me. Our country needs this.'

He nodded, and his minions ended the discussion, forcing Meihu's arm forward. Many soldiers watched attentively, either through interest or fear, as Meihu's fingers flexed away from the cold ice. She must have known what it meant to touch it. It didn't help. Nor did begging her captors for release. None spoke to her. Sabira thought that she saw the sergeant major smiling. Fire ran through Sabira, but there was nothing she could do to stop it. Then the woman's skin touched the Tears of Aderast, and the judge wept with the mountain.

Frost crackled up the woman's arm like it was lightning, accompanied by an inhuman scream. Sabira knew from experience that the judge's mind was now lost in the infinite stream of the glacier, and as the bonding was being conducted so wrongly, all Sabira could do was watch the colonel's latest victim be consumed by it. As the horror happened, though, understanding dawned on her like a bright summer's day. That arm, now thickly coated with ice, sealed it.

She's becoming a yeti, Sabira thought in unison with the frostsliver, horrified.

'End it,' the colonel demanded with cold fury.

A shot rang out, and the body of their forced volunteer fell to the floor limp, staining the rock red with blood. Sergeant Major Lifan lowered his weapon as the discharged smoke floated in the air before him. He looked more affected by the powder stink than the woman he had just killed. The colonel too had other concerns.

'We've tried this ten times now,' he told Lifan, gesturing vaguely at the body that had been a person seconds ago. 'What do they know that we don't? Bonding with pieces didn't work – and as we just saw, bonding with the whole doesn't work. Bonding with males and females, young or old, it doesn't work. There has to be some secret to it. The frost-clerics must have some means of choosing their candidates.'

'Maybe it's the Aderasti blood that makes it work?' the sergeant major said, to the colonel's ire.

'Say that again, if you dare.'

'They probably did something to the glacier. Polluted it, so that it will only bond with their filth.'

This idea seemed to interest the colonel, or at least

to placate him slightly.

'It would be like them to make us the monsters they pretend we are,' he mused, 'but we have no way to test it – and, no, I do not intend to try it myself. If our priests' experiments ever produce a viable embershard I will be the first in line, but until then the damned will be our subjects – until the regiment is rested and we leave for the breakthrough point anyway. It would be fitting to take Adranna with frostslivers, but I'll make do with blasting powder.'

'Aren't the frostslivers the reason we came?' said Lifan.

'And these trials will continue after we have taken the city,' the zealot colonel stated, branded eyes gleaming. 'There will be far more subjects available then. If that doesn't work, we will simply stamp out the bonded. If Ignata cannot have frostslivers, I see no reason to allow others the privilege. If they have sealed our fate, let the Aderasti share it. I may even send a demolitions team all the way down to the glacier source when we are resupplied. Deal with the problem, right from where it wells.'

'Be happy to do that myself, Colonel. Right now, if you want.'

'We haven't the explosives for it right now, I suspect. What we have, we need to break out of Aderast – and I doubt something with as much unnatural power as the glacier can be stopped so easily.

No, were we to bury it in rock, the stuff would simply continue to ooze out from below in some new direction. Our solution must be permanent.'

'Like with Adranna,' said the sergeant major, smiling through the hole in his lip.

'Like with Adranna. Our people will take what they have, as is our right. I saw the conditions they live in, before my family's exile. The Aderasti have their cold paradise while Ignata dies without the magic it justly deserves.'

'You, clean this up,' Lifan told a nearby conscript, pointing to the body and the blood as the colonel drew a pocket watch from his coat.

'We have to act soon. We'll move the powder barrels into place at first light, and prepare for detonation.'

Sabira froze. Yupin was coming for Adranna, and soon. Who knew when it would be first light, in this underground world? These people had to be stopped, somehow. She didn't know what she would have done. Probably something stupid, if it was not for Yupin. He stretched back and clicked his neck as his eyes raked the cave roof. Sabira hurriedly scuffled back, dragging Danlin with her. Too slow.

'Sergeant Major!' Yupin yelled, following it up with more orders, and Sabira knew that bad luck had struck again. He had seen her, she thought, already up and running. Waiting to see how bad things got would only increase the danger. She ran like there were flying snow-spines on her tail.

Danlin was ahead of her, already disappearing into the first tunnel. Not surprising – if he was caught with her, Sabira doubted that he would fare any better. She ran after him, not knowing how long they had before patrols got to them. She was not sticking around to find out, not only for fear of her life, but because she knew now what she had to do.

She was in possession of a terrible secret. Sabira understood what that yeti she had faced really was. What they all were.

They are us and we are them . . .

The frostsliver sounded scared. It didn't like the revelation – but Sabira needed to embrace it. The knowledge meant that there were more yeti in the mountain than she had seen. There had to be, if what she suspected was true. There had to be, if the half-formed plan in her head was going to have any chance. They must have forgotten who they used to be. The people they came from. The duties that they still held.

Sabira was going to remind them.

CHAPTER TWENTY

Sabira could hear doom sounding behind her.

The caves made the sound bounce strangely, and made the hundreds of voices coming from below sound like the roar of a vicious beast.

It would be a while before they reached her and Danlin, but the army had numbers, and time. They could spill through the tunnels without worrying which way was quickest. Eventually they would find her. But if only she could get away, she had the beginnings of a plan...

'I don't think being around you is good for my health!' Danlin said, panting, as she caught him up.

They ran side-by-side. The echoes in the tunnel were growing louder by the second. Danlin pulled them both into an alcove, out of sight.

'I'll lead them away from you,' Danlin said suddenly, to Sabira's surprise.

'You'd really do that?'

It *might just be an opportunity to betray you,* offered the frostsliver, and Sabira glanced at Danlin in suspicion.

'If you don't believe me, pull the trigger,' Danlin said, nodding to the musket in Sabira's hands.

'What?' She looked at him, confused.

'I mean it. Pull it now,' he demanded and took a step towards her. 'There isn't time.'

She left her aim pointed at his leg. Her heart hammered as a bit of metal on the musket pulled back and sprang forward, creating only a click where Sabira had expected a deafening bang.

It wasn't loaded.

'If I'd wanted to fight you, I'd have done it,' he said, smiling.

She felt a burst of warmth for the young soldier. She slung the musket from her shoulder and handed it back to him. 'Thank you. Will you be all right? '

'If they don't find some excuse to whip me to death,' he said, 'I'll do what I can to sow some discord in the ranks. There are others like me. As for the officers, maybe I can convince them that it was just me up on that ledge.' He glanced out of the alcove. 'I've got to go, they'll be catching up.'

Sabira watched as Danlin ran into the passage and turned a corner. Footsteps rushed past soon after and Sabira held her breath, pressed into the shadows.

And then everyone was gone, lost to the mountain's silence.

Sabira hurried back the way she and Danlin had come, listening for sounds of pursuit. There was nothing. The young soldier's plan appeared to have worked.

He was more than I expected. Better. But we can't rely on him.

'Don't count him out yet,' Sabira said, though she could only hope she was right to trust in the soldier.

She thought she knew the way – and the frostsliver helped guide her when she wasn't certain. The moment she saw the passage marked out by the luminous blue mushrooms, she took it.

You're going to get us both killed.

'Why can't you trust me?' Sabira whispered, annoyed.

Because I know what possibility eats at you. Chasing it may kill us both.

'It might,' Sabira agreed. 'But we're going to risk it.'

She continued along the passage, the mushrooms lighting her path. If she was going to die, it would be for a reason, not just in the forlorn hope of survival. It was no longer only about that – or even saving her uncle, no matter how much she wanted to. It was more important than either of them, and Sabira felt sure that Mihnir would see it the same way.

Eventually, Sabira found a tunnel that widened into a full cavern. She stopped, her breath catching in her throat. The cavern towered over her in infinite shades of sapphire. Tunnels led into it from all heights, and Sabira had the impression she was standing at the heart of a warren – or maybe a hive. A yeti hive.

Stomp.

Stomp.

Stomp.

Sabira froze. Heavy footsteps filled the air and echoed around the cavern as yeti strode through the multitude of doorways – almost as if they'd known she was coming, had been waiting for her to arrive. She forced herself to stand still, even though her racing heart screamed at her to run.

Steady. If we are to do this, let us stand tall.

Her legs shook as the yeti moved in closer, their slow approach almost worse than if they had charged her. Sabira's nerve nearly broke. It might have, if it wasn't for the yeti that pushed to the front of the crowd, shouldering between its fellows to reach Sabira first.

It was the yeti with its odd stumping gait that she had faced before. Sabira could see now that one leg was twisted and deformed compared to the other, as if it had not grown correctly.

I . . . I *recognize this one . . .*

Sabira believed it. She suspected that this yeti had been following her, possibly since she had bonded the frostsliver. It had sensed her, watched over her that night in the blizzard, and stayed close, right until it had stopped at the sight of the ash-cat, her childhood toy.

The yeti opened its great fist, revealing the little carving now. It had picked it up, kept it.

Sabira's pulse quickened. She couldn't breathe, could barely think. She was right. The yeti's leg was misshapen for a reason. She looked closer at the large, lumpy limb. Yes – she could see metal rods held in stasis within the translucent icy flesh.

She had known that this moment might come ever since she had realized the yeti were created by a failed bond. She had hoped for it. Feared it.

'Kyran,' she choked, blinking back tears, and reached out her hand.

PART VI

CHAPTER TWENTY-ONE

The creature that had once been her brother loomed over Sabira. Other yeti gathered around, staring down from the upper tunnels. Sabira tried to guess how many were here – there must be hundreds, she thought, as a bead of sweat formed on her brow.

I am sorry. I wish his fate was kinder. He did not deserve this.

She tried to see something in the yeti's face of the boy Kyran had once been, but it was impossible. Still, he was here. That had to mean something, didn't it?

The yeti cried out, its sorrow echoing off the cavern

walls – or was that rage? Sabira didn't know, and from the frostsliver's discomfort, she didn't think it did either.

I *feel them. They are wrong. They are like us, but broken. I see that now. I feel that.*

A moment passed, and Sabira worried that the frostsliver might be right. The others were pressing closer. Curious, or even hungry for this convenient prey that had wandered into their territory? They had killed before. Ignatians, true, but did they know the difference any more?

They were abominations – an unholy melding between human and glacier. People who had tried to bond a frostsliver when their minds were in the wrong state for it. Aderast's gift gone wrong. This was what it meant to fail the bonding. Sabira saw it in the malformed creature that stood before her, the creature that used to be her brother. But she saw something else too: hope.

Another yeti pushed forward, a cold snarl escaping it as it attempted to get to Sabira. She stepped back in fright, but before the monster could reach her, the stump-legged yeti got in front of it, spread its limbs wide and roared into the thing's blank face. Slowly, it moved away. Kyran always was the strongest, bravest big brother she could have hoped to have. Sabira held very still, eyes flicking between the other surrounding creatures until eventually her brother turned his gaze to her again.

'It is really you, isn't it?' she said. She wanted it to be true. She also wanted it to be dead wrong. It had to be true, for everyone's sakes. It was hard to feel that it was, though, when there was so little of her brother visible in the figure before her. Salt stung Sabira's eyes, but she couldn't give in to that. She had to be strong. Until this was all done, she had to hold herself together.

The thing took one more step and reached a paw towards her. She still worried that it might want to do her harm. How could she not when she was faced with a monster of legend? It was almost more than she could bear.

'Please,' she begged in a whisper. 'I'm Sabira. Your little sister. You have to know me.'

He had been trapped in this icy form for months. Even if he recognized her, would that mean anything to him now? He had held her ash-cat talisman through all this, the one that had provided no luck until now. Sabira couldn't think, couldn't breathe. All she could do was hold her hand out to the broken wooden ash-cat and hope.

The yeti's head inclined slightly. Then its icy gauntlet rose and moved towards her. It was close enough to grab Sabira, close enough to crush the life from her.

It didn't. Her glove touched the yeti's open palm, enveloping the figurine, and felt the outsized fingers tense around hers, not in anger, but in comfort. Sabira melted inside. Some spark of him was still in there.

'Thank you,' Sabira said softly.

The audience of yeti shifted, as if all were connected to a single string being pulled. It was the murmur of a crowd witnessing something important.

She wanted to stop there, to let that small contact be enough. To cry. To pull the creature that had once been her brother into a hug. To curse it, and the mountain that made it. Anything, but what she had to do – keep the tension wound up within her, and use it.

Sabira pressed the figurine into the yeti's paw, and stepped back. The creature folded its fist around the precious toy. She let out a noise of pain at the sight, even though she had promised herself that she would bottle it up. Only one, though.

'Adranna needs you, Kyran,' she said, getting control of herself. Then louder, to all the yeti, to every icy face, 'Adranna needs every one of you!'

Would they understand? Could they? She wasn't sure what they were any more – were they protectors of the glacier, as legend had it, or animals with the vaguest memory of being people?

Be ready to run. If you are wrong, there will be little time.

She nodded, and the creatures pressed in closer, watching with their ice eyes. Listening?

'There are men in our mountain,' Sabira said. 'You have seen them. You have even killed some of them.'

The crowd of yeti murmured, a sound like the slow groan of the glacier.

'You may not be men and women any more, but you once had family and homes in Adranna. And you know these men are invaders. You know they mean our people harm.'

She met Kyran's eyes – saw something of him in the blank face.

'They mean our home harm – and they want Aderast's power for themselves! They do not understand that some things are sacred – that some things cannot be stolen!'

The murmuring was rising to a roar. The yeti started to stamp their feet.

The frostsliver flowed into her hand instinctively, an icicle of power glowing in her palm, its frostfire mingling with that of the yeti. 'Join us to fight. Join us to stop the invaders. Join us to save everything that you once loved!'

Then Yeti-Kyran slowly raised one paw into the air above its head and made a noise like the breaking of a great ice sheet. Others followed his lead, filling the cavern until the walls shook with reverberating, resonating sound.

Some part of these creatures knew what they once had been. Perhaps it was just a thread of emotion rather than a memory, but it was enough.

'Can you feel them?' she asked the frostsliver, and it dinged in agreement. 'Then they can feel you too. We can do this!'

As the yeti looked on, Sabira raised her hands above her head in imitation of the yeti's gestures, fingers shaking. After she gave it a mental image, the frost-sliver transformed. A head formed on top of her palms, growing larger and more hideous by the moment, spilling across both her hands. The instant the fake yeti-head was complete it roared too, some-where between the usual chime of the frostsliver and the cracking growls the creatures made.

The yeti's feelings were simple ones. Protect their home. Survive. They weren't so different from Sabira. She latched on to that sense, closing her eyes and pushing it out to the crowd as they pressed in close. *We're the same*, she willed them, *and we are needed*.

Forward! the frostsliver cried.

'Forward!' Sabira shouted.

The frostsliver and Sabira called to Aderast's new army and, as one, the yeti obeyed.

CHAPTER TWENTY-TWO

The yeti followed Sabira as she navigated through the mountain, Yeti-Kyran most receptive of all, striding alongside Sabira at their fore.

You know I feel what you do. I wish it were otherwise, but he is not who he was.

The frostsliver was right – and it was also wrong.

'He's still my brother,' Sabira shot back.

Even so, Sabira couldn't ignore the sound of the creature's stumping gait. That had been her fault, and she was about to pull him and his fellow cursed souls into something worse. Maybe she was no better than the Ignatians.

We are righteous.

'The Ignatians think the same thing,' Sabira replied.

Despite her misgivings, Sabira's heart swelled as she strode on. She felt like one of the legends in the stories, only instead of a travelling bard, or an explorer, or a philosopher, she was a general, marshalling her troops for battle.

At the next open cavern, Sabira called a halt. She shrugged off her pack, deciding that it was better to have mobility rather than what little was left in it. She retrieved the valuable snow-spine stinger, though, tucking it into her belt for safety.

The Ignatians were camped nearby, and she had to think about how to spring the attack. She motioned for the yeti to wait, and crept on ahead, treading softly.

Are you sure that this is what you want to do?

'I didn't think you would object,' she replied silently.

Not to the results, but to the risk. This will be a battle. I am not invincible, and you are not a warrior.

Though Sabira understood, the rebuke stung a little after what they had been through together.

'Frost-clerics have fought before,' she said firmly. 'Bears, and bandits and all sorts.'

True, but you are not a frost-cleric. Tserah and I could have fought many soldiers. You are inexperienced and weakened by everything we have done. I will defend you,

but enough damage will kill even me. I mean no insult –
but there is no shame in knowing your limits.

'No, but there is in giving in to them,' said Sabira
defiantly.

The frostsliver seemed to hesitate. You . . . you are
right.

'I have to . . . wait, what?'

I gave in before when I left Tserah. It wasn't wrong,
what we did, but I did it out of fear, and that was wrong.
This may be our end, and I am still afraid. I know you are
too. But we'll risk it anyway. I am with you – to the end.

Sabira nodded, smiled and crept on, until she could
peek into the Ignatian camp through a crack in the
wall. A few men were on watch and Sabira shrank back
before they could spot her. She was not going to make
the same mistake twice.

If the yeti could surround the area without being
spotted, they could take the Ignatians by surprise.
They weren't the stealthiest of creatures, but if even
half of the plan worked out, it could considerably
improve their odds.

The frostsliver sighed in her head, a tinkling sound
like crystal.

If you're to fight, I suppose you should be armed.

'How about a magic bow?' Sabira suggested to her
bonded partner with a smile.

And fire part of myself at them? Alternatively, you could
chop off your own arm and throw it at the enemy?

Instead, Sabira made do with what she had used before, pausing for a moment to let the frostsliver become a hunting dagger. It didn't look like much.

I *shall make improvements.*

The ice dagger immediately lengthened in Sabira's hand, until it was twice its previous length. She had a sword. She had an army. Sabira was ready to fight.

Sabira waited for the yeti to lumber through side passages and surround the Ignatian camp. She listened, hoping that they had understood her properly, and waited for the first sign of human voices. It came soon enough, when a Ignatian sentry cried out in alarm, screaming about monsters to anyone who would listen.

'Charge!' Sabira yelled, the frostsliver's own icy battle cry ringing between her ears.

Frostsliver blade raised, she pelted away from her forces towards the Ignatians, hoping the yeti wouldn't choose now to abandon her. They didn't, joining the pursuit with surprising speed for creatures that looked so clumsy.

The sight of campfires and shadows appeared around a corner moments later. No going back now. Yeti were pouring from the passages all around, and the air was filled with their roars.

Startled soldiers were roused from eating meals or sleeping, warned by the yelling sentry but not yet understanding the danger. Cook pots were still being stirred, and Sabira could see at the rear of the cavern that the soldiers' blasting-powder barrels remained under guard.

A second after she emerged, the yeti burst out around her, Yeti-Kyran the first to rush to protect her. It was hard to see anything around the storm of limbs, but flashes of panic made their way through to her. Unprepared soldiers hastened to resist the monstrous onslaught, officers shouted orders which blended with the regiment's fear-filled yells.

Stay low!

Sounds of musket fire cut through those cries of alarm, and cold lead raked the great ice beasts. However, the yeti were not so easily destroyed, the musket balls cracking their strange flesh, even embedding within their flexible ice muscles, but penetrating no further.

Sabira found herself letting out a noise somewhere between terrified scream and rousing battle cry as ice chips showered her and her army accelerated, bellowing in wounded rage. The Ignatians could not escape the mountain's unstoppable tide of revenge.

The first of the yeti cannoned into the front line of Ignatians, massive limbs swiping through the crowd. Bodies and blood flew, a score of soldiers snuffed out in a blink. Sabira felt sick at the sight. Images flashed through her head. A burning forest. A whip of glowing metal. A countdown to volleyed musket fire. She dismissed them all, and ploughed on with her people, the frostsliver screaming out,

We are strong! Aderast stands!

The assembled soldiers' discipline broke quickly when faced with creatures twice their size that shrugged off musket blasts. The Ignatians, mostly conscripts, didn't want to be here, and Sabira had been right – they were not interested in laying down their lives for their country. Not like this.

Maybe some of the retreat was due to Danlin's efforts, though she had no way of knowing for sure. Some of the conscripts did find their courage under the threats of their superior officers, forming firing lines. Though chaos reigned all about, the nearest still opened fire, Sabira ducking down in fear of whizzing shot. The rippling blast of the volley rang and echoed, bouncing off the walls in the confines of the cavern.

Though they were tougher than any other living things Sabira had seen, the yeti were not indestructible. One fell under the mass of fire, shards of ice bursting from it where cracks had become full shears. As it died, its huge, solid shell shrank away, the corrupted connection to the glacier dying with it. The body was almost human by the time it hit the ground, more like a bony ice sculpture of a person than the monstrous thing it had become.

Another was brought down, and was not the last. Frostfire battled with the flickers of orange firelight, but the blue was starting to dim. The Ignatians had numbers on their side, and though this battlefield was too cramped to use them well, it was enough to begin slowly whittling down their foes.

Sabira couldn't fight an army on her own, but seeing the yeti die made her want to try. Heart in her mouth, she rushed the nearest Ignatian. He was taking aim at a yeti and not looking at the little girl who couldn't possibly be as dangerous as the monsters, which proved a mistake when Sabira sliced the barrel of his musket in two with the frostsliver. The soldier staggered back and what was left of the weapon went off in his hands. Thankfully, she didn't see what that did to him.

Look out!

Sabira only had time to duck and let out a fearful noise, as the frostsliver turned from weapon to shield in her hand, intercepting incoming fire.

Like the yeti's ice-flesh, the musket rounds did not penetrate the frostsliver easily. Cracks spidered across the surface of the ice at the impact, but then the lead shot was pushed out to clink on to the floor. Sabira only let out her breath when the faults began to seal themselves up – though she could feel the frostsliver's pain, in addition to her body screaming at her.

Forge on – forget me! We have work to do.

She ran, staying low and away from the worst of the fighting. Sabira protected one yeti, and then another from fire, each time fearing that the rounds would break through her defences and rip into her.

It was only after the third time that she realized their mistake. They had kept yeti alive and fighting, but in doing so they'd moved away from the protection of the main group. With a feral cry something attacked her from the side, her shield barely up in time to block a length of scorching heat. Agony exploded through the bond, followed by her own dread when she saw the source.

Sergeant Major Lifan stood there, his broken face half grinning, half raging. He gripped the hilt of his branding lash in a white-knuckled fist, the coil of metal blazing hot. He attacked again, shouting something that might have been 'witch' as the length of scorching words struck the frostsliver again, knocking Sabira to the ground. The bond screamed in her mind, and Sabira thought she might have too.

This was different from the musket rounds that had healed so quickly. Sabira could feel the frostsliver's fear. No wonder – heat was the frostsliver's enemy and that lash represented all that both of them feared the most.

Sabira . . . I'm . . . I can't . . .

She could feel the sizzle in the air as the metal whipped into the frostsliver again and again, melting back the living ice and searing pain into both their minds. It was going to kill them.

Then fire was blotted out by a wall of ice, and the roar of an angry brother.

Sabira stared as the branding lash struck Yeti-Kyran, scoring a line into his skin, though he did not flinch. Lifan whipped him again, snarling, but Yeti-Kyran just turned away from Sabira and charged, massive arms up to defend. He took multiple savage strikes, until his icy body was riddled with burn wounds. Then, to the sergeant major's terrified screams, the yeti was upon him, batting the branding lash free of his hand and grasping hold of the man.

With a roar of victory, the yeti tore the man apart. The motion took only a handful of seconds, but when the yeti was done, it was clear that the sergeant major would never hurt anyone again. Sabira had to look away, though not before making a memory that she would rather not keep. One nightmare had been destroyed by a new one.

Forcing herself to turn to what had once been her brother, Sabira saw a scarred, bloody, damaged creature that could barely stand straight. Its humanity was only a spark, and it was flickering. If she were to count her crimes after this, perhaps turning these wild people of the mountain into warriors might be her worst.

'Thank you, Kyran,' she said, steadying her emotions. She couldn't afford to lose control with the sounds of fighting still ringing in the air. Musket fire sounded nearby and Sabira ran forward, skirting through the battle with Yeti-Kyran at her side, his bulk protecting her from errant gunshots. Her frostsliver took another attack too, and it was only then that she realized how badly injured it was.

There wasn't a bit of the shield that wasn't covered in cracks, and the only communication from the frost-sliver was a pulse of pain through the bond. Sabira tried not to fear what that meant and concentrated on finding something, anything, to end this madness quicker. There, over by the wall of stalagmites through which the glacier was oozing into the cavern, a fleck of gold glinted in the firelight. Two, in fact, attached to the shoulders of the man who had done everything in his power to ruin her. He was directing a small but organized band of men against the yeti's chaotic attacks.

'Colonel Yupin!' she yelled. Every heartbeat that he was distracted was another that the Ignatians were less well organized against the yeti, and another moment that one of them might use to twist his head off.

The man turned at his name, but no yeti attacked him. His eyes narrowed at the sight of Sabira, the only human Aderasti there. He knew she had done this, she could feel it. It didn't matter. Nor did it matter that the frostsliver's injury was leaking through to Sabira, making her heart hammer and stealing her strength. It didn't matter that her injury felt like it might give way at any moment, or that the shield had not properly reformed. She looked to Yeti-Kyran, covered in musket holes and deep lacerations from the branding lash, and knew that this opportunity could not go to waste.

'With me!' she cried, gesturing towards their enemy and pushing every scrap of emotion through the bond and out to her brother.

They charged the colonel together, both siblings wounded, but determined. Yupin fired his musket into Kyran with a horrid snap of ice, but they didn't slow. Sabira felt like she was matching her brother's roar as they smashed into the colonel, sending his spent musket flying and launching the three of them into the stalagmite wall behind.

The rock teeth cracked and broke under the weight of three bodies – one much heavier than the others, and they all went tumbling through. Yeti-Kyran howled in pain, the colonel shouted in shock and Sabira fell with them.

She came through without a scratch, but in that tiny frozen moment held in the air, Sabira saw that there were to be consequences for smashing through a wall of the mountain.

Mainly, that there was no floor on the other side.

CHAPTER TWENTY-THREE

S abira watched emptiness yawning in front of her, thinking her life had ended – before her shoulder impacted on stone, closely followed by her skull. Her ears rang. Dazed, she realized she'd fallen on to a wide ledge that ringed the central opening. From that centre erupted the glowing light of the glacier.

It came from deep below, oozing from the dark in a giant crystalline structure. It wasn't just a column of rough ice here, but a pure, intricate sculpture. It undulated as it rose, forming into symmetrical patterns, like a vast, never-ending snowflake. She got a strange sense of encouragement from it, as if something in it approved of her actions.

The pit was unfathomable, though Sabira knew that somewhere down there was where the Tears of Aderast formed. Where the Deep Explorers had broken the black stones and saved Aderast from its nightmare, if the story was true. Seeing the wonder of the perfectly-formed ice made it easy for Sabira to believe that a god might indeed slumber in the depths.

She wasn't going to learn if it was true, though, not today. Not ever. The frostsliver had collapsed back into the shape of a cracked icicle in her hand, the smaller, now misshapen form apparently less difficult to maintain. Sabira struggled to stand. The frostsliver was in no better condition. Its pain was extreme, but Sabira couldn't tend to it yet.

Both Yeti-Kyran and the colonel had landed near Sabira, the man in bad shape, and the beast in worse. Yeti-Kyran was sprawled over the ledge, at risk of sliding into the abyss, one great arm dangling, his ice flesh wracked with welts from the branding lash.

His ice form was beginning to melt away, and Sabira thought that she could see a hint of the Kyran she had said goodbye to six months ago. Even as she watched him transform, he began to slide further over the edge, too weak to hold himself.

Rushing to his side, Sabira grasped his other arm and hauled on it, but the yeti was too heavy. The arm barely budged. There was nothing she could do. The massive icy paw uncurled, the broken ash-cat figurine that had been gripped in it falling to the ground.

'Hold on!' she demanded, but as she looked into her brother's face, she knew that he could not. He had given everything he had defending her, and Adranna.

It wasn't fair. She had just found him again. Tears filled her eyes. She wanted Kyran back. Why couldn't the mountain give her that, if nothing else?

'Please,' Sabira whispered, though it was no use.

She cried out as his arm slipped from her grasp, and his yeti-body tumbled over the side. She scrambled forward in time to see his icy form, a flawed, imperfect version of a frostsliver bond, fall into the column of the glacier and ripple right into it. Once again, Sabira had been unable to save him.

Kyran was gone.

I am so sorry.

The frostsliver's faint, wounded voice did not help. This time, it really was her fault. It did not temper her grief to know that his sacrifice was for a reason. She stood, staggering. Pain wracked her body, though it was nothing in face of everything else.

What she would have done then, Sabira didn't know. Her emotions were too confused, too raw for thought, and every bit of her, including the frostsliver, hurt. She wasn't given the chance to decide.

'You!'

It was Yupin, climbing to his feet on wobbly legs.

His arm was cut, his clothes torn and covered with rock dust. His eyes were still sharp, still cutting. He advanced on Sabira, drawing a long, vicious knife that reflected the frostfire and looked like it had seen blood before.

'You were on the mountainside when we burnt the forest,' he continued, his inner rage spilling over. 'Did you intend this, even then? Were you laughing at us even as we thought we were hurting you?'

What could Sabira say to that? She laughed in his face – a laugh without mirth, a laugh of pure defiance. Fear had no hold on her now.

'You're all demons!' the colonel yelled. 'Beasts in human form. We'll cleanse you from this mountain and make things right again, witch. My people will be saved, and justice will come to Aderast, I swear it!'

Sabira's rage ignited. 'Adranna was your home!' she screamed at him. 'Why couldn't you just leave us be?'

'Never. Adranna took everything from my family,' he growled. 'The city expelled us, condemned my mother to an early grave. My father to a life of misery. I'm here to take what is my right.' His eyes were full of frostfire and blazing, his breath short and furious. The colonel was well beyond reason – he probably had been for a long time. 'Enough of this!' he said. 'Get out of my way.'

He rushed her, clearly assuming she was harmless, with the frostsliver so injured. He was wrong.

Her eyes wide, Sabira stabbed at him with the frost-sliver. Yupin swatted aside the hand holding the glowing, fragile icicle. He was so much stronger. But as he closed in, his face already alight with triumph, Sabira lashed out with her other hand.

His attack turned clumsy, and he knocked her to the ground with a roar of rage. She sprawled out, rolling over and fearing that she had not done enough. She glanced up at Yupin.

The snow-spine stinger was stuck in his chest, what was left of its venom squeezed into the poisonous man. Yupin was trying to move, but he could not. The rest of his body was a cage for his mind, frozen and useless.

For Aderast, the frostsliver and Sabira thought in unison.

His eyes held a desperate light, skittering from side to side in fear and confusion. For a second he stayed upright, but then the stiffness in his legs buckled, and the colonel toppled backwards, off the ledge and into the abyss.

Sabira wheezed a few relieved breaths, barely able to believe what she had done.

He's gone, she thought. *I'm safe.*

Except that wasn't true. She wasn't safe, not with Kyran really gone, for ever this time. Sabira wanted to mourn her brother properly, after all of this, but as she looked down at the damaged ice chunk of the frostsliver, she realized she could not.

The cracks where the heat had wounded the frost-sliver were not sealing. The emotion leaking through to her from the frostsliver answered Sabira's wordless question. The frostsliver had warned her that it was not invulnerable, and she had not listened.

'I'm sorry. I've killed you. Us,' she said, the hammer of her heart irregular and painful. The frostsliver replied with difficulty,

We did this together. You gave me more time. More time than I deserved. All of it precious.

'You've saved me enough times,' said Sabira, wanting very much to cry.

You could say that I was being selfish. There is no me without you.

'I wish . . . I wish we could have done more together,' Sabira whispered under the blue light of the glacier, as the frostsliver died, and she with it.

This . . . this is not such a bad end. Tserah . . . she would have approved, I think. Maybe even she could be glad that I abandoned her.

That triggered something in Sabira's mind. Suddenly, she knew what she had to do, though she did her best not to let that thought leak to the frostsliver. She didn't want it to try and stop what was necessary.

'Without you, I won't make it,' she said, 'but I transferred your bond to keep you going once before. I can do it again.'

She spoke to convince herself of what had to be done. She would never reach Adranna. When the frostsliver died, Sabira would go with it. There was only one thing left to do. She had already done everything else her body and mind would allow. Adranna had a chance that they hadn't before, and Sabira had been given the opportunity to say good-bye to her brother. It was more than she could have hoped for.

Sabira, no. You don't need . . .

'Thank you for everything,' Sabira said, cutting her companion off and forcing herself up to stand unsteadily, facing the fractal pillar of the glacier. The place where the frostsliver had been born. The place that Sabira would die. She let her last emotions fill the bond, knowing that it was too late for the frostsliver to intervene.

Fighting back the fear, she reached out and drove the fractured, burnt splinter that was the frostsliver into the ice column, knowing the sacrifice that she was making. This was going to be her end, down in the dark where no one would ever learn her fate.

Then the storm was upon her again, the torrent of the glacier in her mind. The thing that made it, the vast thing deep beneath the world pulled on the one bonded to her, tearing it away with unbelievable force. She wanted to hold on to it, but knew that she could not. Letting the frostsliver go was the only way to save it. Maybe Tserah and her partner would be reunited in the mountain. If so, Sabira would be joining them soon.

With a last wordless goodbye, the frostsliver slipped away from her, a droplet running back into a lake. Back to the thing that slumbered below. Back to the infinite shoal of other frostslivers. Many of many once more.

Sabira felt her sense of self fade. The glacier was ripping her apart, or the loss of the frostsliver was destroying her. Nothing made sense except that she was going to end in this primal stream of force.

Then there was something in that torrent that Sabira recognized, and not the frostsliver she had been bonded with. That cluster of consciousness had faded into the greater swell, with no more than an echo to tell Sabira that she had ever known it.

Only briefly had Sabira known the other presence before, and then she had brushed against its mind only lightly. Her time with Tserah's frostsliver had put her mental senses to the whetstone, and she saw now not an unknown sliver of the glacier, but one cut from ice by her hand days before.

It had been there on the mountainside with her as the avalanche fell, before it was lost to her and absorbed back into the glacier. Sabira knew now that it had been with her since, flowing back through the current of the Tears of Aderast, a calming presence watching from behind glass as Sabira travelled down into the mountain.

It came to her, chose her as she chose it – bonded with it, giving up all of herself to the mighty flow of the glacier. All that sensation pushed into her and through her and suddenly, she knew that she was not going to die.

The rush began to fade, and the world worked its fingers back into Sabira. This wasn't the blackout harshness that she had experienced the first time, but more like coming up into warm air from freezing water. As the maelstrom of the Tears of Aderast fled from her, a whisper of voices spoke. Tserah. The frostsliver. Kyran. All gave her the same message that she had been told before, and with many times the feeling behind it.

'Live well, little ash-cat.'

Live well, my partner.

'Live well,' they told her in unison, and then Sabira sat panting on the ledge once more, dazzled by the brilliance of the glacier column.

At her neck, a pleasantly heavy cylinder of ice touched her skin, its caress both warm and cold. Not her partner in this mission through the mountain – that frostsliver was gone, returned to be with the one its bond was strongest with. No, this was her own frostsliver, and with it Sabira felt strong like she never had before. Another time, she might have revelled in it, but after such loss, and with their trial not over, her frostsliver rippled into action.

Work remained to be done, and they were ready for it.

CHAPTER TWENTY-FOUR

Her new frostsliver was not like the old. Tserah's partner had been wise to the ways of humans, having watched them for years through the cleric's eyes. This one was raw and wild, full of desire to be one with Sabira.

It did not appear to understand language, or if it did, it did not yet know how to speak it. Sabira didn't need words to make her meaning clear. Her emotions were unmistakable.

She sent her new companion an image of what she needed from it, feeling the strength of the bond that the second, more controlled touch with the glacier

246

had bestowed on her.

Her frostsliver began spilling from its place at her neck, tendrils of ice spreading rapidly across Sabira's clothing. It was like the brace, but everywhere. Ice webbed into complicated lattices, like bone and muscle on top of her own, but impossibly thin and complex beyond sight, a brilliant, beautiful thing of solid magic.

Her frostsliver encased her entire body, armouring Sabira against the world. Even her head was protected, in a helm that covered all but her eyes. She felt strong, like a real warrior, despite her armour being thin as paper.

The power pushed at her, and the sounds of battle called, her injured knee no longer holding her back. She left the wooden ash-cat lying where it was, a token of remembrance for the brother she'd lost, backing away and holding up a hand of goodbye to the glacier, as well as those she left with it. She broke into a run, found it faster than she had ever known, and made for the ruined wall back to the Ignatians and danger.

For Mihnir. For Tserah and her frostsliver. For Kyran.

Sabira leapt from the pit, heart racing. The strength that she now had access to was incredible, though she could still feel the stress it was putting on her body.

Something truly had changed with that second plunge into the glacier's power. Maybe she had been doubly charged with magic by the experience, or maybe it was just that Sabira had changed, was far from the girl who had first bonded with Tserah's frostsliver.

Her frostsliver hummed through the bond. It had been born in battle, and seemed pleased to be obeying Sabira's commands. She scanned her armoured head across the cavern, taking in the state of the fight, her heart pounding like a drum.

As she watched, her heart sank. Rebellion was in full flow, with conscripts battling officers – and each other – all around. Danlin had done everything he had promised and more, though maybe the chaos of the yeti attack had done just as much to set the Ignatians against each other. But Sabira could see that the effort wasn't going to be enough.

The yeti's numbers had dwindled, brought down by weight of musket shot, and the resistance within the Ignatian ranks was disorganized. It wouldn't last. Loyal soldiers of the Ignatian army still outnumbered the rebels and yeti combined.

The battle here might buy Adranna a day or two – maybe even shift the odds a fraction in the defender's favour, but as long as the loyal Ignatians still had the blasting powder ...

The blasting powder! It was the Ignatians' strength, but also their weakness, though they didn't yet know it. She ran for where it was stored, knowing it was Adranna's only chance.

Sabira sprinted the distance, effortlessly slicing apart two muskets in passing using a blade extruded from her armour. This was for Adranna. There would be a price, but it needed to be paid – even if the price was her life. And Mihnir's. And Kyran's. Her eyes stung with tears. They'd fought so hard to survive, and now . . .

She skidded to a halt by the alcove and saw that the space inside was stacked with several dozen barrels, each labelled with the same danger symbol. Sabira didn't know much about blasting powder, though she had heard enough to guess what this could do. She doubted this was the full amount intended for Adranna's walls, but it would have to be enough.

No naked flame burnt near the barrels, and even the heavy lanterns were set well away from them, as if the objects could barely stand being in the same space as each other. The real reason, of course, was to eliminate the risk of one being knocked over and creating some-thing cataclysmic.

Sabira was going to be that cataclysm.

It wasn't a good thought. It meant killing who knew how many people to save many more. The idea of so many entombed in the mountain horrified her. On top of that, might this risk another avalanche? Probably not, so soon after the first, but the thought was still a grim one.

What was worse – to take the risk and doom so

many people, or to fail to act and watch many more suffer at their hands?

Cursing again at having to make the surgeon's choice, Sabira forced herself to action. This was a decision that was going to haunt her either way, and she would rather make all this death worth something, if it was possible.

She pushed over a barrel and put a hole in one end with a frostsliver spike, allowing the powder within to spill free. It pooled next to the other barrels, and lengthened into a trail as Sabira used her new strength to drag it along. A musket shot glanced off her armour as she waddled backwards out of the cache, and her hands shook, but she did not drop her precious cargo, and everyone was too distracted to stop her.

She pulled the barrel as far into the battle as she dared, and then gave it a shove to roll it back the way it had come, its purpose served. Now, how to light her fuse? She'd have to go back for one of those lanterns to smash.

Just as she was about to, a familiar face came running out of the melee. Danlin fired his musket wildly behind him with one hand as he sprinted at her, causing him to drop it. That didn't slow him down, though, and he kept on going at full pelt.

'Sabira!' he yelled, leaping her powder trail, and heaving something glowing hot at her. She let out a squeak of fear, and then realized what Danlin had delivered to her. Sabira reached out and caught the still-hot branding lash by its handle. It was just a thing now, no longer to be feared. Not when she was about to make use of it like this.

'You're going to finish this, right?' he asked, sounding worried. She noticed he had a straight line of blood on his face from a graze above his eye – he'd come a finger's width from death. She nodded and said,

'Run – get somewhere safe, if you can!'

'Give them hell!' Danlin shouted, and sprinted away. Watching his retreating back, she hesitated. Could she survive this? Was she doing the right thing? Would the explosion be enough to destroy this army? Would her actions accidentally harm her people? Would the glacier, even as ancient and powerful as it was, be able to survive the damage? Her frostsliver thrummed with power, and Sabira found strength in it. She hadn't been given an answer, but she knew it all the same.

She touched off the apocalypse.

Sabira dropped the branding lash into the trail and sprinted away, pursued by the angry hiss of burning blasting powder. She had no idea if there was a safe range, let alone how long she had to get to it.

Chaos was everywhere, the battle slowed but not ended. Pockets of violence assaulted her senses with the cracks of firearms, animal roars and screams of pain. Most of the yeti had given their lives for the place they had once called home, but some still remained.

'Run!' Sabira yelled at them, waving her arms. A few followed, and even some of the Ignatians took the hint.

Seconds later, the mountain turned to ash around her.

She had expected it to match the deafening roar of the avalanche for volume. It did, and more. Though she had clamped armoured hands tightly over armoured ears, the blast hit like a hammer blow. The wave of sound was torture on her eardrums.

A pulse seemed to go through the stone under her feet, as fire bloomed behind her, followed by a cloud of dust. Then the real destruction began, starting with the ground Sabira stood on, which split sideways.

Part of the ceiling crashed down, and more followed as Sabira stumbled and pushed onwards, unable to see beyond her face and hearing nothing but whispered screams and ringing in her ears.

She caught a glimpse of the still-flowing glacier as she moved, and in a flash wondered if it would still be able to make its way upwards through the mountain after this.

Sabira ran, with no idea where she was going, or if there would be a surface under her feet when she got there. Dust obscured everything. If Danlin and those with him were alive, Sabira had no idea where they were. She feared for them, but could do nothing.

Sabira caught sight of black shapes running in front of her, heading for what she thought might be the main entrance to the cavern. Should she risk following? She had no idea if they were friend or foe.

She was not given the choice.

The ground gave way, sending both Sabira and the unfortunate soldiers tumbling into darkness. Rocks thudded painfully into her, with the force to kill someone less armoured, and then she was in freefall.

The void enveloped her until there was nothing except her and her frostsliver armour glowing in the black. Then she bounced off something hard, causing her head to spin. More things hit her, or she them – she didn't know which – and Sabira heard screams from people faring worse than her.

Then something smacked into her entire front – the ground, she thought dazedly – and the world stopped moving. Most of it anyway. Rocks ten times her size crashed on top of her, and only through surviving that did she realize that she had lodged into a fissure at the bottom of the hole. She had no idea how far she had fallen, but squirming on to her back hurt enough for it to have been half the height of the mountain.

It certainly looked as if half of it had come down after her, and the way it was shifting made Sabira worry that it hadn't finished yet. There were more ominous rumbles, as well as impacts on the rubble that

253

pressed on Sabira's tiny spot of safety. She raised her arms, as if they might defend her, waiting for the groaning mass of stone to give way. It did not. The rocks settled, eased together, and lay still – at least for the moment.

She wormed back on to her front and squinted through the stinging haze of debris the blast had kicked up. There was a way out, or at least down – a thin hole, to be sure, but Sabira thanked the mountain for her luck all the same.

Heart pumping blood around her body so fast she thought her head might explode, Sabira scrambled in. There might be only a moment or two before everything collapsed.

The delicate-looking armour of her frostsliver caught and snagged as she pushed her way down, but soon the crack widened enough for her to walk. Ominous cracking noises from behind kept her moving, and the passage actually lurched further apart, some stress on the rock pulling the fissure wider. Sabira had no way of knowing if there was anything at the end, or if this new passage would be her prison, sealed and filled in behind her with the remains of the caverns she had destroyed.

She was barely able to see which way was up, until she saw something ahead in the dust and smoke, a thin band where the light was different. A wall, with a slice of space in it.

Coughing, Sabira stumbled towards it. It looked like there was a way through, but not one wide enough for a person. Her fingers could pry their way in, though not the rest of her. She pulled back, generating a new frostsliver blade, refusing to be denied.

One way or another, this was the end. The choking dust might suffocate her, or her frostsliver's power might rip her heart open – or she might finally be free.

Sabira sliced at the rock again and again, and jagged stones were stripped away with every strike. Blood pulsed in her ears with the effort, but the threat of her body giving out did nothing to stop her. With every swing, her frostsliver pushed just as hard, its near-delight in the act keeping them both going.

When she couldn't do any more, when her head felt on the verge of bursting, Sabira pulled back and slammed into the crack in the wall, unwilling to stay in the half-collapsed tunnel a moment longer. She burst through the weakened stone in a plume of dust.

She let out a scream and skidded to a wobbling halt. Too much haste. After everything she had been through, that was what almost killed her. Pebbles and bits of broken rock tumbled away from the ledge Sabira found herself on, trailed by billowing dust.

It was a long way down.

She swayed, blinked and balanced, every nerve on fire. It was hard to concentrate through her lack of breath. She had to force down the impulse to fight and run. The frostsliver began to pull back from her body, and finally Sabira's pulse slowed a fraction, allowing her to focus on what was below.

For a dreadful moment, the world looked just as blank as it had a moment before. Could this be just another cave? No, there were pinpricks of light in the blackness above. It was no cave. It was night time, with stars welcoming her back to the world. Sabira had made it. She was free of the mountain.

That was Adranna down there, and the lights of the city were the most welcome sight of Sabira's life. From what she could tell in the dark, its walls looked as if they had taken a beating, with great drifts of snow built up against them, but the gates had been mostly cleared.

Sabira saw the bright paints of the murals, lit by the lamps strung along the walls, and knew them for home. The fresh air hit her then, the sweetest, most vital thing Sabira had ever tasted.

It had been so long since she'd had this kind of relief. Her mind couldn't take it in, and Sabira's body suddenly refused to be pushed any further. She fell into a sitting position on the high ledge she found herself on, four or five storeys up Adranna's rear wall.

For days – or a lifetime – she had been pushed to her breaking point. Now it dropped upon her with a great weight. Like her frostsliver, Sabira was struck dumb. Her senses faded to dullness, but not before she felt her cheeks grow wet. Were they tears of happiness, or sorrow? She did not know.

A voice yelled up to her. A friendly one, full of concern. Was that a question on the wind?

She couldn't reply. Could barely understand what was being asked. Sabira's mind was a thick bank of fog, and nothing would penetrate it. Almost nothing. Something was moving below. People, maybe. Shouting. Meaningless words. Not quite. Through her stupor, Sabira managed to comprehend one thing that was enough to make her smile through her tears. Those people saw her, and were coming.

They were coming to bring her home.

CHAPTER TWENTY-FIVE

Peace. That was all Sabira wanted. Was it so much to ask? She was in bed, resting in the temple with a beautiful greenhouse garden outside her window, for the mountain's sake. Surely that should be sanctuary, if nowhere else was.

'All returning bonded usually face certain mental trials,' the red-robed man at the side of her bed told her. He was one of the many healers who had seen to her. What was his name? Harten? Hadaten? It didn't matter.

'Oh, yes?' Sabira said icily. Her frostsliver dinged in righteous anger in her head, backing her up.

She had saved the city.

If only Sabira could end her tale with that thought, but there were too many loose ends – and too many regrets. The frost-clerics kept trying to make her face them. Now they were trying to get her to face these trials too.

'Yes, it's been tradition to ensure that the bonding produced a stable pair, one able to take on the rigours that will be asked of them in life.'

Sabira politely told him where she was going to put her frostsliver if anyone asked again. She had already been through enough to prove herself.

'Perhaps . . . perhaps you have a point,' he admitted. 'Though, if ever you change your mind, the temple will always be open to you.'

It had been a good place to recover, with the expert knowledge of the frost-clerics helping her heal, and the stream of visitors coming to wish her well. Many of them she didn't even know, and after a while it had become too much. Then her mother had kicked up a fuss, and the visits had been limited to family and healers only, to Sabira's great relief.

'In fact, you must be thinking about what comes next for you,' the frost-cleric said. 'You could always join our number. Of course, that would prevent you from joining the council at some later date, but that's not necessarily a bad thing. A life of devotion can be just as rewarding as a life of influence.'

Sabira looked up at the ceiling of her room, hoping to escape into it. They had given her a very nice room, with only one other bed, and that one had been kept free of other patients for her comfort. The frost-cleric wasn't going away.

'I'm not sure that I want to join any group of people that kept so many secrets from the rest of us,' said Sabira, hoping that he might take the hint. They must have known. All those frost-clerics studying the glacier, taking people to bond to it. Some hint of what it could do must have slipped free. Why else would they test people?

'Well,' he said, 'we only had suspicions about the yeti, never confirmation. However, now the word is out. Everyone's heard your tale, though not everyone believes it. It would perhaps have been better to have kept that part private. Still, we must make the best of things.'

That knowledge was going to be hard for Adranna to take in. Sabira suspected that opinions in the city would be sharply divided as to what to do about it. She was still conflicted. Kyran. His name kept running through her like lightning, hurting every time it came to her.

'Well, maybe if you'd told people your suspicions, it wouldn't have been such a shock,' she said, more strongly than she really meant it. She understood why they hadn't. People might have begun to fear the glacier – or even frostslivers, and that wouldn't be right.

'Perhaps I should leave you,' the frost-cleric suggested. 'Your leg is doing well, and the rest of you will be fighting fit sooner than you could believe. I'll see you again at your next check-up.'

He rose and patted down his red robes.

The mountain is in your debt.

The tinkling at his neckline was a little deeper than Sabira's frostsliver. She mustered a weak smile, but no more. Both man and frostsliver exited, and shut the door behind them.

Once they were gone, Sabira relaxed back and opened herself to the bond. Her frostsliver still didn't use words, but its feelings were easy to lean on. They mirrored her, filled her in where she needed it, and let her lose herself in the flow.

Feeling slightly better, Sabira flexed her leg, sending a twinge through her body. Painful, but maybe she ought to thank the mountain that she had not lost more. After all, she had been luckier than Tserah – and Uncle Mihnir too.

At her insistence, a party of Aderasti, including her father, had made the climb up the bonding path to assess the damage to the mountain stairs and, though it was not said so starkly, to recover Tserah and Mihnir's corpses. She would have gone too, if not for her enforced period of recovery. They should be back soon, she thought, and her stomach knotted again.

She was distracted by the opening of her chamber's door. If that frost-cleric was back to try and ask more foolish questions, she didn't know what she would do. He wasn't. It was Danlin, wearing light Aderasti clothes instead of the tar-smelling uniform of the Ignatian army.

Though he was covered in cuts and bruises, they had healed a little since Sabira had last seen him. Danlin had crawled out of the mountain half a day after Sabira, leading a small group of like-minded conscripts who had also managed to survive the disaster she'd inflicted on them.

'Hey,' he said, taking the stool the frost-cleric had vacated.

'Hey,' said Sabira. 'How's it going?'

'Can't complain. They've treated me well here. Everyone else too, and they didn't have to. Even helped some people who don't really deserve it.'

'They're frost-clerics. They'd say that everyone deserves help. Even your officers,' Sabira suggested.

'Well, in that case, I'm just glad that the officers are probably all dead – though a few are apparently still missing. Lots of other conscripts too, but I bet those left are more interested in deserting than in forming up to fight.'

Sabira nodded. It would be weeks before the last of them were winkled out of the mountain, but they had been coming in dribs and drabs, most surrendering to the mass of Aderasti who now guarded the tiny entrance to the tunnel system from hastily-constructed platforms. Those who didn't found that even superior weapons were no use when they could only fight one against many.

'I won't cry over that,' said Sabira.

She had no desire to go near that crack in the mountain – she had too many bad memories. She had been having nightmares, in fact, and it didn't seem like they were going away. There was hope, though, and days ago Sabira had not had any. Her daylight hours were much improved, and the shaking and confusion that had accompanied the end of her ordeal had mostly abated.

'You feeling any better?' Danlin asked, as if reading her mind. Sabira made a noncommittal noise. She didn't want to lie, but she wasn't ready to speak her mind yet either. He didn't push the issue, instead adding,

'I'm getting out of here today. City council says I and those I vouch for can go free.'

'Quite the responsibility,' said Sabira.

'Ha, it's obvious that they don't know me at all.'

She laughed, with more humour than he seemed to find in it, and said,

'I think they might have got the measure of you better than you think.'

Danlin cocked his head in confusion. Sabira let her words hang on their own. She'd seen enough of him now to know that there'd be no living with him if she started giving him actual compliments. Seeing that she wasn't going to explain, he said,

'It's funny – now I've got my freedom, I don't quite know where to go with it.'

No smile accompanied the words. He must be serious, and Sabira could see why. His kind weren't exactly trusted in the city. Sabira's good words had gone a long way, and they had been given better options than other soldiers who had once been their fellows, but that only went so far. They couldn't go back to Ignata either – they would be shot as deserters – and those like Danlin who came from the colonies had no home to return to there anyway.

'You know,' Sabira said slowly, 'you should go and find my mother. Tell her I said you need somewhere to live – until you know where you want to be, I mean.'

'She seems a bit . . . ah . . . scary?'

They'd seen each other during visits a couple of times.

'If she doesn't react well,' Sabira said with a smile, 'tell her I told you to say that her daughter wouldn't be alive without you, and maybe she ought to be grateful. I don't think you'll need to, though. She takes her responsibilities seriously – we Aderasti don't refuse hospitality to people who need it.'

'A fact that a few of my friends are going to be very glad of,' Danlin said. 'Though I don't know how good a solution it's going to be long term.'

'One more problem for the list, when news gets back to Ignata,' Sabira agreed. 'I just hope the High Tribunal doesn't side with that man's ideas.'

'Doesn't seem likely, with him murdering Judge Meihu,' said Danlin, not needing to be told who 'that man' was.

'I guess we'll have to wait and see,' Sabira replied.

'I guess.'

They sat quietly for a little while, slightly awkward, but not so much that either of them chose to end it. It was ended for them, when the door banged open, making both of them jump.

Through it came two men hauling a stretcher, and then, to Sabira's delight, her father, wrapped up in heavy furs. He must have just got back from the climb, but that meant . . .

'Sabira,' the lump of furs on the stretcher groaned, to Sabira's astonishment. 'Knew they made the right choice with you.'

'Mihnir, you keep that mouth shut and rest!' said her father, and the man was hustled over to the room's second bed to be relocated and made comfortable. As the stretcher-bearers did so and made their way out, Sabira's father came to her side, and said,

'He's lost four toes and two fingers to frostbite, half

his muscle and fat to starvation. Had to operate up there in that cave of yours! He probably won't be working as a packman again – frankly, it's a miracle he made it at all.'

'Oh, leave off, Rabten,' Mihnir muttered to his brother.

'Hush. Sleep,' he was told. 'I said it was a miracle. Don't throw it away.'

Sabira had to agree, as an unstoppable grin spread across her face. Apparently, nothing could kill that man.

'He's going to be all right? After that?!' Danlin said, not being all that tactful, as Sabira was coming to expect from him. Her father turned to the young Ignatian with the slightest hint of suspicion, saying,

'And you are?'

'This is Danlin, Father,' Sabira had to explain. Her father's face softened immediately, and he actually darted forward to envelop Danlin in a heartfelt hug, stunning the Ignatian into silence.

'Young man, I'm very glad to meet you. You must come and meet the rest of the family. A feast is the absolute least we can do for you.'

'Well, actually . . .' Danlin said, obviously thinking of the earlier conversation. Sabira let him off the hook by saying diplomatically,

'Shall we leave that for a bit, Father? I'd like to take a minute to enjoy Uncle Mihnir being alive!'

'Just about,' mumbled the other bed, with surprising good humour. They all laughed, though there was a little edge to it. This had been the closest of calls for Mihnir.

As the conversation deepened, with Danlin properly introducing himself to Sabira's two relatives, she found herself thinking that this was what real sanctuary should be. People coming together, discovering the bridges between them that they didn't know they had.

It put her in mind of a question she had been asking herself for what seemed like all of her years. What was she going to do with her life? Seeing these people together, Aderasti and Ignatian, Sabira found that her mind was starting to be made up.

EPILOGUE: AFTER THE MOUNTAIN

Two weeks later, Sabira finally walked out of the temple.

She hadn't healed completely, but the rest of her injuries would not be helped by bed rest. Only her knee had been done permanent damage – she would have a small limp for the rest of her life without her frostsliver's assistance. A small price to pay.

What happened inside Aderast still had its hooks in her. She was thinking of it as she descended the temple's intricately-carved steps, though her family was waiting for her at the bottom. Danlin stood self-consciously with them, as if wondering whether he was imposing.

How could the sight of them not make her think of the face that was missing, and forever would be? Both her parents wore another ribbon on their arms again, but blue instead of red, which was no tradition she had heard of. They hadn't talked to Sabira about it, but she thought that it might be in remembrance of both their son and the frostsliver that had saved their daughter's life.

Kyran was truly gone now. It was where he had been heading from the moment that he chose to ascend the bonding path alone. For her, it felt a little easier now that she knew. Sabira had seen what had befallen him, and had seen that her brother had loved her until the end. For him, though? She could not say.

Maybe becoming a yeti hadn't been so bad – a simpler life for creatures that only just remembered their humanity. Then again, maybe that existence had been a curse he was glad to break. Sabira would never know. He was with the glacier now, and in a way, that had been what he always wanted.

Mihnir was missing too, back in the temple with a longer recovery ahead of him. He grumbled about it constantly, as her uncle always did when he was sick, but after what he'd been through it was better than anyone could have hoped for.

It was a clear day, clearer than most Sabira had known. She reached the bottom of the stairs under bright sun, with not a hint of snow. Yet the embraces her family gave her, and the awkward handshake Danlin supplied, were far warmer than the mountain climate's tepid sunlight.

Sabira reached up to touch the glow at her neck, a reminder of all that the mountain was, and what she had to be. Blue, dancing frostfire. The cause of, and solution to, so much. It called people to action – terrible, great, or both.

'Danlin's been teaching me all about his chemical science,' Sabira's father said, interrupting her reflection.

'Has he?' Sabira asked, looking at the ex-soldier.

'Nearly blew up my skinning area,' her mother said with a hint of sullenness.

'Come now, dear, the boy said it was safe,' her father said, the peacemaker once more. 'At least after that last ingredient got added anyway.'

Looking sheepish, Danlin took a step closer. He seemed less talkative than he had been under the mountain, but Sabira didn't blame him – his world had been upended too.

'Would be nice if our nations could be soothed like a chemic reaction,' he said quietly.

Sabira thought of the fanatic, Yupin, and the angry words she had heard from some Aderasti since her return. The colonel had succeeded in one way, in making resentment fester. Hating that he had got even that far, she said, 'I wish it was so easy.'

As she spoke, Sabira wondered why it wasn't. Couldn't the two peoples find a middle ground? The Ignatians were wrong to try and take what wasn't theirs, but wasn't ignoring their troubles wrong too?

There had been too much history for easy answers. She knew that, but Sabira also knew that if no one tried, then there was no chance of a solution. That was why she was going to.

Sabira had never expected it, but in the end her purpose had found her. War might not have come to Adranna this time, but at least some Ignatians must feel as Yupin did – there would be more opportunities for bloodshed in the months ahead. She was going to pour all her energies into making those opportunities vanish for ever. Alone it would be impossible, but . . .

We are together.

The sudden tinkle of her frostsliver speaking aloud startled her family. Sabira smiled. She was starting to enjoy that reaction. The frostsliver had begun speaking during her recovery, though rarely, and she had already become glad of its voice.

'Sure,' she said, and took her first step into tomorrow, her family at her side and laughter on the breeze. Her life would not remain so easy, for Sabira knew that she had mountains of work ahead.

Sabira swore to Aderast that one day she would be welcomed to Ignata as a friend, and Danlin would finally return home in peace. It might be a lifetime's work, Sabira thought, in concert with the approving chime of her frostsliver.

It would be a lifetime well spent.

ACKNOWLEDGEMENTS

I've got a lot of people to thank, so I'll get right into it.

The *Times*/Chicken House Competition brought *Frostfire* to the world, so I thank everyone behind it, especially Barry Cunningham for deciding that I was worth taking a chance on.

Kesia Lupo, for being the first at Chicken House to see the book's potential, and for her editing, which has improved *Frostfire* many times over.

Rachel Leyshon for further editorial advice and suggesting structural changes that absolutely were the right thing to do.

Laura Myers, Lucy Horrocks, Jenny Glencross and Sue Cook for your attention to detail during the production and proofreading stages, and without whom so many mistakes would have slipped through.

Jazz Bartlett and Laura Smythe for publicizing the book, using your own kinds of arcane wizardry.

Elinor Bagenal and Sarah Wilson for your tireless work on rights and getting *Frostfire* in front of as many people as possible, no matter the place or language.

Rachel Hickman for commissioning *Frostfire*'s fantastic cover, designed by Steve Wells and illustrated by Karl James Mountford – whose excellent talent I can only hope to see more of on my future books.

Elizabeth Smith, Paul Smith, Lola Collishaw, Rita Piper and Rebecca Hall, for being willing to read *Frostfire* back when it was *Frostsliver*, and far wordier than it needed to be. Without your advice and encouragement, these words might not be in print now.

And finally, I come to you, reader. If you're not one of the people mentioned above, thanks for taking enough of an interest to read all the way to the bitter end. If you've enjoyed this book, can I trouble you to ask that you consider reviewing *Frostfire* on your favourite online book retailer? If you're willing, then you too truly deserve your place in these acknowledgements – you wouldn't believe how much difference a few good reviews can make.

In any case, you can find me and all my future projects online at JHBSmith.com or on Twitter @JamieHBSmith.

THE LAST CHANCE HOTEL by NICKI THORNTON

Seth is the oppressed kitchen boy at the remote Last Chance Hotel, owned by the nasty Bunn family. His only friend is his black cat, Nightshade. But when a strange gathering of magicians arrives for dinner, kindly Dr Thallomius is poisoned by Seth's special dessert. A locked-room murder investigation ensues – and Seth is the main suspect.

The funny thing is, he's innocent . . . can he solve the mystery and clear his name, especially when magic's afoot?

A jolly, atmospheric mystery.
THE TIMES

Hercule Poirot meets Harry Potter in this mind-bending, magical, murder mystery.
MISS CLEVELAND IS READING

Paperback, ISBN 978-1-911077-67-1, £6.99 • ebook, 978-1-911490-41-8, £6.99

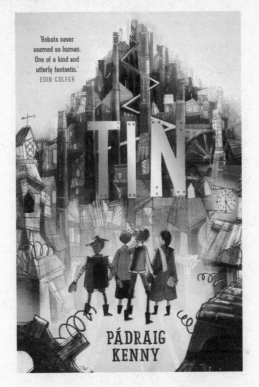

'Robots never seemed so human. One of a kind and utterly fantastic.'
EOIN COLFER

TIN by PÁDRAIG KENNY

Orphan Christopher works for Mr Absalom, an engineer of mechanical children. He's happy being the only 'real' boy among his scrap-metal buddies made from bits and bobs – until an accident reveals an awful truth. What follows is a remarkable adventure as the friends set out to discover who and what they are, and even what it means to be human.

Robots never seemed so human. One of a kind and utterly fantastic.
EOIN COLFER

Paperback, ISBN 978-1-911077-65-7, £6.99 • ebook, 978-1-911490-09-8, £6.99